THE CEO & I

RIVER LAURENT

The CEO & I
Published by River Laurent
Copyright © 2017 by River Laurent

ISBN: 978-1-911608-08-0

APPRECIATION

Thank you Leonora Elliotte and Brittany Urbaniak

CHAPTER 1

LUKE

He's fucking flirting with her!

Fury slams into my head. The guy at the immigration counter continues to look her up and down. Then the smarmy bastard lifts his eyebrow in a completely inappropriate way. My hand clenches the handle of my briefcase to stop myself from going over to him, knocking his head off, and shoving it up his—

Jesus H. Christ!

Where the hell did that come from?

Jade Emerson is not my girlfriend. She's my damn PA! She works under me, scratch that, for me. Plus, she's married. I *never* mix business with pleasure. And she is the last person to turn my head. I'm pretty certain that I've never met a woman who is more determined to look like someone's grandmother. Coke bottle glasses, not a lick of makeup, severe bun, dowdy clothes. She's got it all. The works.

Although, to be honest, her utter lack of sex appeal was one of the reasons I hired her. I make it a point not to work with attractive women. I didn't always have that line in the sand, but I'm thirty-four now, and I've bedded enough women to know the score.

Basically, I'm sex on a stick.

That's not bragging or conceit. It's just the way things are. I see the looks I get from women when I walk by. Their eyes widen, their lips part, and they focus on me like nothing else in the world exists. Throw in the fact I'm filthy rich into the equation and suddenly, I'm irresistible. That's fine outside of the office, but in an office environment, it's a damn nightmare.

I want to keep things strictly professional. Partly, because I don't need that kind of complication, but mostly, I just don't want to be the guy who bangs his secretary. I find the whole idea sleazy and vulgar. It's not who I am.

Hiring married, dowdy women like Jade Emerson makes it easy to stick to my rule. Even if they are the type to cheat on the side, they understand I'm not in their league. It's great for me too; I'll never be distracted or tempted. Sure, some men might find her sexy. Notice the reaction of the fool at the counter, but not me. My type runs to models, 'it' girls, or just straight up bimbos. At least, this is how it's supposed to work in theory. And how it has worked for the last two months she's been with me.

Peanuts for brains returns her passport and she hurries to join me. My theory has worked for the last two months and there is no reason it should not work for the foreseeable future. Deliberately, I glower at her.

"Sorry, it took so long," she says meekly, tucking her passport into her purse.

"Try to keep up, Mrs. Emerson." Turning on my heel, I start striding away. I can hear her sensible librarian shoes clacking on the polished floor as she jogs alongside. I know I'm being an ass, but I'm still reeling from the crazy moment in my head when I got all possessive over her.

My nostrils flare suddenly. "What's that smell?"

She blushes. "One of the stewardesses spilled the fish surprise on me."

Now, I can't help staring at the color seeping up her neck and into her cheeks. I frown with irritation. I'm losing it. What's wrong with me? Sure, I've been working flat out all week and I was exhausted before the nineteen-hour flight from New York, but this just isn't me. I don't lust after my secretaries. Especially, plain Janes like her.

I glance at her brown turtle-neck top. "We're in Bangkok. Why are you dressed as if we are on a trip to Alaska?"

"Uh...huh, I thought it might be cold in the hotel," she mutters, her eyes sliding away.

I shake my head and carry on walking towards baggage claim. *Just forget it, Luke.* She is some other man's problem.

The airport is ultra-modern and clean, but it's packed with travelers, clogging up the walkways in the terminal. Although, the crowd parts easily in front of me. I tower over most of the people here. They move out of my way like I'm going to knock them over if they don't. It's not far from the truth. I feel impatient and restless. I put it down to the fact that I've got a lot riding on this trip.

"Did you confirm our reservations for this evening?"

"Yes. Table for six. Nami. 8.00 p.m."

I nod with satisfaction. "Good. If we land these Japanese clients, it'll be our first step toward breaking into the Asian markets. An entire hemisphere of untapped potential, ripe for the taking will open up."

"Yes, Mr. Remington."

"What's on tomorrow?"

She checks her phone. "You're scheduled to be at the economic conference for the seminar on Developing New Business Markets in the morning at Conference Room Chakrii. It starts at eight, but the two speakers you were interested in listening to, start at nine and eleven respectively. You have an hour to kill in between, so I've scheduled for you to meet with Mr. Dimitriou who has flown in specially from Singapore for that meeting."

"Great. Is lunch with Carl still on?"

"Yes, at one. I've booked a table at the Golden Orchid restaurant."

I nod. "You will be joining us, right?"

"If you need me?"

"Yes, I do. You'll have to take some notes."

"I'll change the reservation."

"My session is after lunch?"

"That's right. Your presentation is at 2.30 p.m."

"You brought the slides for it?"

4

"They're in my suitcase."

"Good." I run my hand along the back of my neck. The airport is fully conditioned and I am already sweating. "What am I doing after that?"

"It'll be 4.00 p.m. by then. I thought you might want some free time to rest, or do some sightseeing."

I spear her with a disapproving look. "Mrs. Emerson, this isn't a vacation. I didn't get where I am in the world by taking it easy and walking around like a goddamn tourist. We're here to work. See about scheduling something for tomorrow evening with the Norwegian delegation. I don't want any down time while I'm out here. Might as well seize every opportunity we can."

"I just thought—"

"Well, stop thinking. Let me do that. Your job is to keep my life running smoothly, so I can think. Speaking of which, go grab our bags. I need to make a call."

She scampers off obediently, and for a second I stare at her ass, even though it is impossible to tell what it actually looks like under all the layers of clothes she wears. Today, she is wearing a pant suit. It's a nice suit. Very professional. The problem is it's at least two sizes too big for her. She practically swims inside the fabric. Like a kid wearing her mother's clothes.

Her choice of clothing is quite incredible. Once she came to work in a grey suit that was so meritless and ugly I nearly said something, but I managed to hold back. Her fashion choices are none my business.

I chuck her out of my head and call head office in New York.

There are a couple of deals being negotiated that need my input. I give the senior vice president his instructions, and hang up just as my PA rushes back, rolling both our bags on either side of her.

Her face is flushed with exertion and despite the thick lenses of her glasses, I see dark circles under her eyes. I guess it can't have been much fun for her travelling in coach with screaming babies all around her and the air stewardess spilling fish sauce on her. I consider saying something nice, but I bite the comment back. Our relationship is perfect at the moment. Jade Emerson is without doubt one of the best PA's I've ever had, and I'm damned if I'm going to ruin it.

We get out of the airport and the heat slams into me. It's like being in a sauna. "Where's the driver?" I ask her impatiently.

She looks around, concerned. "He should be here."

"Well, I don't see anyone with a placard with my name on it."

"They use iPads for that now," she murmurs.

"Whatever they use," I say irritably.

She pulls her phone from her pocket. "Let me call and find out what's going on."

I cross my arms impatiently, as she begins speaking to someone on the other end of the line. "No, that's not what I emailed," she says calmly. "I'm sorry your driver wasted his time by coming here an hour ago, but if you take the time to check my email, you'll see that I sent the correct instructions and the flight was neither delayed nor early." She pauses. "How long will it take you to organize another car?" She listens then frowns. "No, we can't wait here for an hour. I'll find alternative arrangements. For the record, I'll be

6

expecting a refund of the payment I have already made." The other person raises his voice and she listens to him ranting with pursed lips. Two months with her is enough to know that means she's dealing with an asshole, but she's just too professional to stoop to his level.

Anger rises up in me. I can be hard on her, but I won't stand by and let someone treat her like shit. She doesn't deserve that. "Is everything, alright?" I ask her.

"No, but I can handle it," she says, holding the phone slightly away from her ear.

"I know you can handle it," I say, meaning it. "It's not you I'm referring to. It's the asshole on the other end." I extend my hand to her. "Give me the phone."

I can tell from her slight hesitation that she doesn't want to, but she knows better than to disobey a direct order from me. She passes the phone to me.

I put it to my ear.

By now, the man on the phone is not just yelling, he's going ape-shit. His accent is thick, but I make out 'stupid fucking bitch' just fine.

This is the point where I cut him off. "Stop speaking. Now."

He is so shocked he stops mid-sentence.

"Now, I don't know who the fuck you think you are, speaking to my assistant that way, but you've gone way over the line. If you were here in person, I would teach you a lesson in manners. And if I didn't have better things to do with my time, I'd go down there personally to see that you never speak to a woman that way again."

"Sir, I apologize for—"

"Did I say you could fucking talk?"

The man goes completely silent for a moment, before making the mistake of opening his trap again. "No, sir, but—"

"Here's what's going to happen. I'm going to hang up this phone. Then I'm going to spread the word to all my associates that your car service is blacklisted. If I were a betting man, I'd say the majority of your clients are business-men. Well, not anymore. You might want to start looking for a new job now." I hang up before he can say anything else.

She is staring at me wide-eyed.

I hand her phone back to her. "Too much?" I ask.

A slow smile spreads across her face. "Could be, but he was an asshole."

"Send an email to all your friends about these guys."

She cocks her head in confusion. "My friends?"

"Well, not your friends, exactly. But all the other assistants to *my* friends. The ones you deal with on a daily basis. Tell them never to use this car service again. Whatever the hell it's called. Maybe then our friend will learn a bit of humility."

She nods. "I will. And, Mr. Remington?"

"What is it, Mrs. Emerson?"

"Thank you," she says.

I shoot her a tight smile. "No one treats you that way. Not while I'm around. Now go find us an ordinary cab, but make sure it's air-conditioned."

CHAPTER 2

LUKE

The gap-toothed cab driver sings softly to himself as he navigates through the hellish traffic of downtown Bangkok. He has a lousy voice, but I vastly prefer it to any forced attempt at small talk. I know they're just angling for a better tip. The joke's on them. I tip so much better when they say nothing at all.

I look out of my window. Bangkok never changes. Tall buildings, temples, golden Buddha statues everywhere, busy sidewalks, men and women in colorful clothes. Even where we are now, stuck in traffic, there are enough glimpses into Bangkok's Asian culture to make the place feel exotic and mysterious. At least, that's how it felt the first time I came here.

But travel the world enough and nothing really surprises you anymore. I've traveled a lot, seen a lot, and done a lot. This is the first trip I am taking with my PA. I think I heard one of the managers mention that this might even been her first trip abroad. All of this must be so new to her.

I turn to look at her.

She is leaning forward and gazing out the windows, her eyes wide and shining. I follow her gaze and look at the shops passing by. For a moment, it's like I'm seeing the world through her eyes. The city is vibrant and alive. The way it had been when I first came here. Young and starry-eyed. Yes, Bangkok has a way of making the rest of the world seem dull and gray.

My eyes stray back to her face.

She looks almost beautiful in her excitement. I find myself staring. Seeing her from the side, without her glasses in the way, is a revelation—her eyes are quite stunning. I thought they were brown, probably because I've never paid much attention. Now I see they're an extraordinary hazel. The mixture of green, brown and gold glow in the sunlight, and for a timeless second, I'm captivated.

Then I disgustedly shake myself from my thoughts and remind myself this is Mrs. Emerson. My married PA. Yes, I care about her, but not like that. Never like that.

Suddenly, the silence becomes awkward for me, and I need to say something. Anything. "So I take it this is your first time in Thailand?"

She turns to look at me, a warm, open smile on her face. It transforms her. "It is," she admits. "I never knew how beautiful it is."

"If you think this is beautiful, you should see outside the city. It's unlike anywhere else."

She sighs. "I'd love to, but this isn't a vacation, remember?"

I smile at the way she throws my words from earlier back in my face. I wouldn't let most people get away with that, but for some weird reason I let her. "No, it's not. But maybe you can find some time in the schedule tomorrow and the day after to look around."

"Will you join me?" Then adds quickly, "I'd be nervous to wander around alone."

I shake my head. "I'll be far too busy, but you arrange for a tour guide to show you around. I'll pick up the cost"

Her look of excitement deflates. "If you're working, I'm working."

I can't argue with that. She is my right hand. I need her at my side. I can't do the things I want to do if she's not around. Still, she deserves to enjoy herself too. She works hard for me without complaint. I could give a little back. I make a mental note to figure out one fun thing for her on this trip. If I have time.

We get to the hotel. It is five-star accommodation from top to bottom. We're given the VIP treatment and very quickly booked in by smiling super-efficient staff and taken up to the Tower Club suite on the fifty-sixth floor. Technically, my PA and I will be sharing the space, but the suite is big enough for her to have her own bedroom and bathroom. I want her close, not on top of me.

The lounge is a picture of luxury. A bottle of champagne and a platter of fruit and cheese is waiting on a glass table. The bellhop carries our luggage into our respective rooms. Mine has a king-size bed and hers is a single. I walk to the wall to ceiling window and look down at the view of the entire city with the river running through it like a snake. In the late afternoon sun it is quite something, but Asia also look its best at night, when you can't see the dust and the grime. Then it will be breathtaking. The windows are triple glazed, so no sounds permeate it and it is almost hypnotic to watch the hectic world so far below in complete silence.

"Excellent choice on the hotel," I say.

"Thank you, Mr. Remington."

I turn away from the window and clap my hands together. "Right. Dinner is in three hours. Just enough time to clean up, do some work, and get ready. I'll grab you at quarter to eight?"

She nods. "I'll be ready. Let me know if you need anything else in the meantime."

I go into my room and close the door on her.

The first thing I do is call down to housekeeping to pick up my suit and shirt to make sure they are pressed and presentable for tonight. It's not that I'm worried about my appearance. Of course, I take care of myself, but I'm far from vain. Tonight though, I need to show our potential Japanese clients my best side.

Business culture in Japan is a complicated affair, but one thing I know for sure...they are an incredibly thin-skinned lot. Little things matter to them. Even something like cursorily glancing at someone's business before putting it away into your pocket will be taken as a lack of respect for that person's title and rank. No, you've got to carefully study it and nod approvingly before putting it away. Showing up in a rumpled suit would be considered offensive.

I peel my shirt away from my sticky skin and wash away the sticky heat of Bangkok in the shower. Feeling refreshed and blissfully cool after a shave, I come back to my bedroom. I have two hours to kill so I lounge on the bed in my boxer briefs, and start going through my pitch to my Japanese clients.

It is then I hear the scream.

In the blissful silence of triple glazed windows, the sound is piercingly loud. My papers slide off my lap as I leap off the bed. Sprinting across the lounge, I throw open my secretary's bedroom door, and skid to a stop. She's standing in the middle of the room clutching a small towel to her. She spins around and stutters, "Luke...I mean, Mr. Remington."

"What is it?" I ask, staring at her in disbelief. She is not wearing her glasses, her hair is cascading down her back, and her legs are long and deliciously smooth. I don't know why, but I thought she'd have hairy legs. I blink. Damn it.

She points a shaking finger towards the bathroom.

Tearing my eyes away from her dripping body, I stride over to the bathroom and look inside. "What? I don't see anything," I say, looking around the empty bathroom.

"Look in the tub. There's a huge freaking spider in it."

"Is that all?" I ask, relieved. Hell, the way she screamed, I thought someone was stabbing her to death with a rusty knife.

"Is that all?" she counters, her voice rising hysterically. "Go and see it. That—thing is a monster."

"Don't be such a baby," I reply as I move to the tub and look inside. It's bright blue, furry, the size of a goddamn softball. "Shit. That *is* big."

"I told you," she cries fearfully. "I can't believe I was in there with that—thing. It looks like a tarantula had sex with a smurf."

My back is to her, so I didn't have to hide my smile, but seriously, the spiders in the tropics are something else. "I'm sure he was just trying to get a peek at you," I tease. "Don't worry. I'll take care of this little peeping Tom." I go back out to my room and grab one of my shoes. I return and it is still trying to climb the slippery sides of the bath. *Alright, you little pervert. No more ogling my sexy assistant.* The arthropod makes a squashing sound. Wadding up some toilet paper in my hand I scoop up the blob that looks like crushed blueberries. I flush its remains down the toilet, chuck my splattered shoe in the trashcan, and turn around.

"Problem solved."

She is watching me from the door with just her head poking around the door frame. Her hair is hanging in wet waves around her face. "Are you sure?"

I roll my eyes. "Yes, I'm sure. It's all safe now."

She takes a step into the bathroom and time freezes.

She still has a towel wrapped around her, but just barely. It's too small. In her haste to escape the shower, she must have grabbed the wrong towel. The fabric clings to her wet skin, leaving very little to the imagination.

The swell of her breasts under the towel is shocking. They look ripe and full, and I fight a wild urge to reach out and touch them. A bead of water drips down her neck between her breasts. My eyes follow it. Fuck, there's a lot of cleavage there. If the towel were an inch lower, I'd see everything.

I had no idea she hid such amazing tits beneath her baggy outfits.

I follow the curve of her body down from her breasts to her hips, then down to her exposed thighs. Her skin is creamy and flawless. I want to taste every inch of it.

The edge of the towel comes down to the top of her legs, barely hiding her pussy from my hungry gaze. Somehow, I feel like this is more seductive than if she'd been completely naked. She's revealing so much but not really showing anything at all. It was a tease. A turn on. My insides clench with desire, and I feel my cock stir in my boxers.

I look up at her face quickly, not wanting her to see me eye-fucking her. Again, I'm taken by surprise at how gorgeous she looks. Her long dark hair is no longer in the too-tight bun she always wears. It falls to her shoulders in waves.

And without her glasses, her eyes enchant me. I caught a hint of it in the cab ride over, but seeing her up close like this is like getting hit by lightning.

It was the first time I've ever seen her. *Really* seen her. She's been hiding her sexy body from the world under those terrible outfits. Or maybe she's been hiding it from me. Either way, it's a shame. A woman this fine needs to show it all off. To hide it is a crime. It's like keeping the Mona Lisa covered up under sackcloth. The world deserves to see it.

Jade Emerson is a masterpiece!

I can't reconcile the two versions of her. My plain assistant can't possibly be the woman standing in front of me. She looks like her mind-blowingly hotter, younger sister.

All of these thoughts run through my mind in a matter of seconds. Even then, it feels like I've stared too long. I'm not shy when it comes to letting a woman know how much I appreciate the sight of her, but this is my married PA. And I always keep things professional between me and my secretaries. I'm not going to stop now.

Our eyes meet.

Something like an electrical charge crackles in the air between us. I wonder if she feels it, too. Probably not. She called me in here to kill a spider, not so I could take advantage of the situation and stare at her almost naked body.

At that moment, I become distinctly aware that I'm only wearing my boxer briefs. I don't mind showing off my body. I take care of myself for that very reason. But the sight of Jade Emerson's alluring figure is having a physical effect on me.

I'm not rock hard yet, but I'm getting there. I need to cut the tension or things between us are going to get really awkward. I have to say something. Anything. Just to get my mind off how good she looks. To distract that animal part of my brain that is screaming at me to throw her against the wall and fuck her senseless.

That is, of course, after I rip the towel off and see what other beautiful secrets she's been hiding from me, and running my tongue over every inch of her...until she begs me to let her come.

Shit, this isn't helping.

I have to think of something, but the only thing my brain can think about is how goddamn hot she is. So I go with that. I clear my throat to make sure she can't hear the desire in my voice. "So, Jade. You're looking different."

She peers down at herself and her cheeks turn red. "Yeah, it'—a-a I'm not wearing any clothes."

"It's a good look for you."

Her head jerks up and she looks at me in surprise. "Mr. Remington?"

I force a smile and raise my hands in a placating gesture. "That came out wrong."

It's not that I'm nervous. In fact, it's the opposite. The fact that I find her so attractive has kicked my sex drive into gear. I *want* to butter her up. I *want* to take things to a sexual place. That's my natural instinct in a situation like this.

I'm stumbling over my words because I'm fighting those instincts. I'm trying to keep things from changing between us. No matter how much my cock is telling me to let it happen. "What I mean is..." I pause. It's getting way too hot in this bathroom. "How do I say this without totally pissing you off?"

She bites her lower lip. "Just say it."

My eyes drift over her one more time and I have to force myself not to lick my lips. "Fine. You're very attractive."

Her mouth gapes open, those sensual green-gold eyes wide, but I've already started. There's no stopping now. The water is dripping down, drop by drop, over the arch of her neck and all I want to do is lick it off. I'm sporting a full hard-on by now. This is all so insane. I clear my throat. "I'm not hitting on you. I'm just saying this as a fact. Normally, at work, you dress in such unflattering clothes, and you keep your hair wrapped in a schoolmarm bun all the time. With a couple of new outfits and a new hairstyle, you'd be a hell of a looker."

Her eyes grow troubled. "I know that," she says.

I'm surprised by her response. "What do you mean, you know?"

She shrugs, and her towel shifts in a very distracting way. "I'm not stupid, Mr. Remington. I know how to dress myself."

I stare at her, trying to understand what she's saying. "Wait, so you dress that way on purpose? Why would you want to make yourself unattractive?"

Her eyes lock with mine. "Because of you."

CHAPTER 3

JADE

"What do you mean it's because of me?" he asks, with narrowed eyes.

Oh, shit. I didn't mean to blurt that out to him. Usually, I'm calm, cool, and professional, the perfect assistant. I can keep my head on straight even in the most difficult scenarios, but I feel almost dizzy from the buzz of my near-death experience, and my present situation, which can only be described as bizarre.

Up until a few moments ago, my boss has not seen me in anything that has even hinted at my figure underneath. Now, I'm standing in front of him in a towel that barely covers me. Actually, it's so small I'm afraid even to move. Any shift could be disastrous.

This is bad, but that's not what has my cheeks flushed with heat. It's the eye-popping fact that he is near nude himself. All he's got on is a pair of distracting-as-hell boxer briefs. Let me say, right away, they leave nothing to the imagination.

I always knew he was in great shape, but to actually see him like this? The man is a fucking god. His body is rock solid. Layers upon layers of lean muscles. One on top of another. Every one chiseled and perfectly defined, flexing beneath his inked skin with every little movement. It's quite impossible not to stare. And I haven't even got to that muscle bulging inside his underwear.

Holy crap is it big or what? Nah, it has to be a trick of the light, or I'm still in shock. No one is that honking big. Still...I can almost feel the heft of it just by looking. Slickness forms between my legs that has nothing to do with the shower I just took. I tear my eyes away and meet his waiting eyes. I take a few seconds to take stock.

1. We're both seeing a lot of more of each other than we've ever seen before.

2. I definitely like what I see which, of course is, besides the point, since...

3. He has just made it very clear that while he thinks I'm attractive in a detached, objective way, he's in no way hitting on me.

4. Even after taking the massive hard-on into consideration, I have to agree with him. He's not hitting on me. I'm not his type. I've seen some of the women he goes out with. They are so stunningly gorgeous, they make you want to give up and die or open up another packet of Oreos.

So really, no actual harm has been done. And if I play this right, I could stop drowning inside ugly smocks that my grandmother wouldn't wear and ditch those plastic glasses.

I lick my lips apprehensively. "I wanted to tell you, but I'm worried it will piss you off."

"Mrs. Emerson," he says, his voice low and deep. "Whatever you have to say, just say it. Yes, I might get mad. I can't promise I won't, but I *can* promise I'll get totally pissed off if you don't tell me."

I nod and raise one hand in a placating gesture. "Fine. You have a reputation, okay?"

"A reputation?" he echoes with a frown. "You're going to have to be more specific. A reputation for what?"

"The agency that sent me to work for you. The woman there warned me about you before I came in for the interview."

He crosses his arms over his chest. His muscles tense and flex.

Okay, now, I am gulping for air.

"What in the hell did they warn you about? I'm not dangerous," he says staring at me like he wants to punch something.

My body is trembling with nerves and if I keep going, there's no telling how he'll react, but I have no choice as I've come this far. Might as well go all the way. "They didn't say you were dangerous. They told me you won't hire women that are even remotely attractive or unmarried."

He nods thoughtfully. "They're not wrong. I didn't know other people knew about that, though. I've never said anything to anyone. It's a personal rule."

"I guess other people noticed. The woman told me it was because all these young girls end up falling in love with you and acting unprofessional. And they're distracting to you. So I made sure to dress as frumpily as I could to get the job."

Luke stares at nothing, like he's lost in thought. His expression is unreadable. I assume this is the calm before the storm and brace myself for the inevitable explosion of anger. It doesn't come. Instead, his blue eyes bore into mine, trapping me in his gaze. "Are you even married?" he asks in a deathly calm voice, which is even more chilling than when he is throwing a tantrum.

"No," I confess, before quickly adding, "I'm good at what I do, Mr. Remington, so I don't see why my marital status, or appearance should prevent me from performing a job that I am perfectly qualified for."

For a few seconds more, Luke continues staring at me. Then he throws his head back and laughs. "That was clever, Miss. Emerson," he says. "Well played. Whoever that woman is at the staffing service, she was absolutely right. I wouldn't have hired you if I knew what you really looked like."

My stomach flutters at his words. He thinks I'm pretty! Suddenly, I'm conscious again, of how naked we both are. "I'm sorry, sir. I didn't mean to lie to you. I just really need this job."

He waves my apology away. "Are you kidding? You saw a problem, and you found a creative solution. I like that. What's that old saying? Dress for the job you want. In this case, the job you wanted required you to dress like a clueless librarian."

"So you're not mad?" I ask tentatively.

He laughs again.

The sound is deep and rich. It sends waves of warmth echoing through my body.

"Not at all." He steps toward me. "You're a good assistant. I would have missed out on hiring you if you hadn't done what you did. You found a way around my rule, and I'm glad you did."

"About that rule," I say, clutching my towel hard. "What's that about?"

He dips his chin. "I'm a man of big appetites, Jade. When I see something I want, I claim it. That goes for business and for pleasure, but I try to keep those two worlds separate. At work, I need to be focused and professional. No distractions."

"Sure," I reply, trying to hide the quaver in my voice.

"I'm not immune to the charms of beautiful woman. It's only natural. And look at me." He gestures at his body.

Well, since he's giving permission...I quickly take the opportunity to stroke him with my eyes. Mmm.

He continues, "I'm a good-looking guy, so it's only natural that women gravitate to me too, but it's a recipe for disaster if I satisfy my needs with one of my employees, things get complicated quickly. So that's why I have my rule."

"But I've seen a few pretty girls in the company."

"They don't work for me directly. The rule only applies to women I work closely with on a daily basis. Like my personal assistant." He looks me up and down, not hiding what he's doing. "We'll be spending a lot of time together, Jade. A lot of late nights. A lot of one-on-one meetings. I can't have that kind of temptation around."

My heart skips a beat and refuses to steady. Did I just hear what I heard? I laugh nervously. "Good thing, I'll never be a problem like that, then. I'm not really your type."

He takes a step closer to me.

Instantly, I feel the heat from his body drying my skin.

"That's where you're wrong. Right now, you are extremely...tempting."

His words send a shiver through me. My nipples harden beneath the towel. His eyes lock with mine, sending an electric current through me. "Mr. Remington—"

"Luke," he says softly.

My lips part and I feel my chest tightening.

He frowns suddenly and looks away. "Good thing we have too much to do on this trip to get distracted. Finish getting ready. We need to be on top of our game tonight."

With that, he exits my bedroom and closes the door behind him.

I collapse on the bed, groaning.

What the hell just happened?

Oh. My. God. He asked me to call him Luke.

My heart hammers away as conflicting emotions war inside me. Luke knows what I look like now. He knows having me as his assistant violates his unspoken rule, but he just behaved as if it isn't that big a deal. Like I am such a good assistant, my little trick doesn't matter. Will he change his mind once he's had some time to think about it? Will he decide to fire me? Or will he just transfer me to another department?

On the other hand, I'm over the moon that Luke knows what I look like now. I hated dressing like a frump, I hated the thick glasses, hated scraping my hair into the most unattractive hairstyle anyone could ever have, and I sorely missed my lipstick and my mascara. It did my ego no good to be so invisible for so many hours of the day. So, I had to be nearly naked for him to notice me, but he has finally looked up and noticed that I'm a woman. He even said I'm tempting. My heart feels as if it will fly out of my body with happiness because obviously, I've been crushing on him hard since the first time we met for my job interview.

I mean, I'd have to be blind not to be attracted to him.

I was barely able to string a sentence together during my interview with him. Who can blame me? The man is the sexiest thing on two legs I've ever seen. Dark tousled hair, ruggedly handsome face, strong cheekbones often peppered with sexy stubble. And his eyes. Oh my, those eyes. They're so blue it's like looking into a hot summer sky. Sometimes, when he's explaining something to me, he'll look directly at me, and I can feel the intensity of his gaze. It cuts through me, like he's looking straight into my soul. Intoxicating me.

I'd even say that over the past two months, my crush has deepened into a kind of obsession. When he's talking to other people, I find myself just watching him, greedily drinking in the sight of him.

I didn't think it was possible to find him any more attractive than I already did. Suits were made for that body and face. That is, until I saw him just now, when he stood in only his underwear and told me I was tempting. It's enough to make my head spin with desire.

Then the way he'd looked at me before he left. Intense. I'm still reeling from it. I honestly thought he would kiss me, or throw me on the bed and claim me. I wish he had. I hug myself and remember the delicious tension that hung between us. I felt it. I wonder if he felt it too. I think he did. He'd never looked at me that way before. And he'd said more than once that I am attractive. Distracting even. I smile to myself.

Too bad, he hadn't acted on those feelings.

I make my way back to the bathroom and look around me. The spider is gone now. All that's left is a dark blue smudge. I hate spiders with a passion, but this one was a bit of a martyr. It gave up its life to change mine. I wonder how on earth it got into the bath. Maybe it hitched a ride on of the cleaner's carts. I think of Luke slamming it with his shoe. Luke took care of me. Warmth fills my belly. My hero.

It's like at the airport earlier, when that guy from the car service was being a dick and I couldn't be a bitch back because Luke was standing in front of me. Luke took care of that for me, too. I'm no damsel in distress. I don't need a man to save me, but it feels amazing when the man who comes to my aid is Luke.

Dreamily and completely forgetting that I've already had my shower, I step into the tub. The water rushes over me while I carry on fantasizing about him. Yes, he is an asshole some-times. He's over the top and domineering, and when it comes to work he is tough and demanding, but he never lets anyone else treat me badly. He may never have noticed me as a woman, but he's always been protective of me.

It's one of the things I love about him. His protective streak is all the more endearing because he has no ulterior motive for it. Until today, he never looked at me with any kind of sexual interest. So he didn't protect me because he wants to get in my pants. He did it because that's just who he was. Good and kind. Otherwise, why would he give a damn how other people treat me?

I sigh and reach for the soap.

But Luke is more than that. He's complicated. A mystery. The more time I spend with him, the more I realize how much I don't know about him. His past. His family. What he wants for the future.

I know I shouldn't but I want to feel his hands run over my skin the way the water from the shower does. It's a dream that can only bring heartache. I'll become like all those other secretaries who made the pathetic mistake of falling in love with someone like Luke Remington, but I can't stop myself from wanting his eyes to lock with mine like they did just before he went back to his room. Wanting to see the bulge growing between his legs and know it's because of me.

Thoughts of Luke have my core aching with desire. A desperate, overwhelming need claws at me, urging me to do something about it. I consider taking matters into my own hands. It will be a long, frustrating night with Luke if I don't relieve the pressure building up inside me.

But I don't have time.

I have to start getting dressed soon. The last thing I want is to be late. I finish cleaning up and get out of the shower. I dry myself off and walk over to the closet where I've hung my clothes. I need to pick an outfit for tonight's meeting. Of course, I brought a lot of clothes with me. I like being prepared for anything. If it rains. If it's suddenly cold. If I need to sit on my own by a swimming pool. If I go trekking. If I have some free time to go dancing with some of the other conference attendees.

I browse through my collection of grey and brown pant suits. They helped me land this job by hiding my body, but now that my secret is out, the idea of wearing one of them seems silly. Luke knows what I look like now. Do I really have to hide myself any longer?

I slide my suits aside and look at the one thing I've never worn around Luke. A dress. This is my if 'Luke is not around and I slip out into the balmy night looking for adventure' dress. Yeah, right, but in my head I am full of fun and adventurous. Emerald green and sophisticated.

It isn't particularly sexy, but it fits right, accentuating my curvy assets. It's emerald green and it really makes my eyes pop. I wonder if Luke will like it. It's a classy dress. Neither too slutty or showy. It's the kind of thing I'd wear to dinner with business clients if I was in a different job, one that didn't require me to hide my figure.

Indecision tears at me. Will Luke be mad if I dress differently tonight? Will it make things stranger than they already are?

Screw it.

I don't want to hide anymore. Luke knows what I look like now. No sense in pretending I'm that same old frumpy girl with a bun. I'm ditching my bun and wearing my dress.

I look forward to literally and figuratively letting my hair down for one evening. I deserve to have a little fun. I'm in a foreign country, I don't have to hide the way I look, and I get to spend an evening with Luke. I may as well do it right.

I blow dry my hair and leave it in shining waves down my back. I put on some makeup, more than I've ever worn around Luke, actually accentuating my features instead of toning them down. I leave my glasses sitting on the night-stand by the bed and dab perfume at my pulse points. Then I slip into my daring open-toed shoes.

When Luke knocks on my door, I open the door and his jaw almost hits the floor.

CHAPTER 4

LUKE

"Holy shit," I mutter.

Jade smiles at me. "Is that good or bad?"

"Good. Damn good." I look her up and down, mesmerized. "It's just a surprise. That's all."

She lifts an eyebrow at me. "A bigger surprise than seeing me in a towel?"

"Actually, yes," I reply. It's not just the clingy dress that snags my interest, although it certainly did. But her face looks so different, too. She's done something different with her makeup. It's not like she painted on a new face. No, the differences are subtle, but powerful. "No glasses tonight?" I ask.

"No. Actually, I have a confession to make."

"Let me guess."

"Yup. I don't actually need glasses," she says, her lips curving up in a wicked grin. "I took your advice."

"My advice?"

She nods. "You told me to try new outfits and to change my hair. So I did."

"Yes, you did," I say slowly, still unable to tear my eyes from her luscious curves. "I just didn't expect the change to happen so soon."

She shrugs, making her breasts jiggle enticingly. "Why wait? The cat's out of the bag. No sense in going back to my baggy old clothes." She leans forward conspiratorially.

I now get a waft of her perfume mixed with the smell of skin.

"I hated them with all my heart," she admits.

"I'm sure you did," I answer automatically. I'm too overwhelmed by the sucker punch delivered by her scent for my brain to work.

She looks at me from under her lashes and smiles slowly.

I shake my head in disbelief. "Who the hell *are* you, Jade Emerson?"

"Maybe it's time for you to find out."

"Maybe," I say softly.

She sucks her bottom lip into her mouth.

At this action my cock twitches with interest. "Come on," I urge impatiently. "We don't want to be late."

"Good idea," she agrees and starts walking in front of me.

My eyes rove over her body and ass freely, now that she can't see me looking. Her hips sway enticingly below her trim waist, hypnotizing me, keeping my eyes glued to it.

Heat flares inside me. Jade had been sexy in just a towel, but now she blows me away with how hot she looks. It's like the woman who disappeared into her hotel room never came back out. This is someone else. Someone irresistible.

Even in her previous life, I guess I've always secretly found her attractive. She was always more than her baggy sweaters and her thick glasses. There'd always been a spark there. A hint of some sexual magnetism, but I'd always been able to ignore those stirrings. I'm not sure I can ignore them anymore.

We step into the elevator and I hit the button marked L.

Jade stands beside me, looking straight ahead, and saying nothing.

Since I don't want to ogle her directly, I stare at her reflection on the mirrored walls of the elevator.

Her full, ripe breasts swell against the bodice of her dress. She's not showing a lot of cleavage, but somehow, it's one of the sexiest damn dresses I've ever seen. It's like the towel. It shows off everything while revealing nothing.

My cock throbs in my pants. I shift my suit jacket to hide my growing erection. I close my eyes to shut the image of her out of my head. *Control yourself, dammit. Stop gawking at her like a hormonal teenager.*

Even with my eyes shut, I still see her. In my imagination, I'm there, too. I'm pressed up against her from behind. My hands slide up her dress, up her smooth, flawless skin. All the way up. Until my fingers encounter wet folds.

I open my eyes before things go too far. Jade is my assistant. I can't have these thoughts about her. She's been strong enough to keep things between us professional. I'd be smart to do the same.

I swore I'd never be so crass as to seduce my assistant. It's cheap and tawdry. Not because she's beneath me or anything like that. It's because I don't want to be *that* guy. I refuse to be the cliché businessman who takes advantage of his secretary. I'm not that. I won't be that.

Deep down, this is the real reason I had my rule. Not to protect me from them, but to protect them from me. And in a way, to protect me from myself.

I enjoy sex. I'm not ashamed of that fact. The problem is, once I see a woman I really, really want, I have to have her. It's a compulsion, a burning need that won't go away until it's satisfied.

Now, I want Jade.

We sit beside each other in the limo on the way to the restaurant. Night has fallen over Bangkok and the world outside our windows is lit by glowing storefronts and neon signs. The lights paint her face in shifting colors, giving her an ethereal quality. Almost like she's not real.

Nothing feels real now, not since she emerged from her room as this vision of beauty. She's thrown my world off-balance. I can't concentrate. I can't get my thoughts in order. I can't even pry my eyes away from her.

I have no idea how I'm going to get through this meeting with the clients. I'm too distracted. Jade is the only thing I can think about right now. The rest of my world has faded. She's the only thing in focus.

If these potential clients weren't so important, I'd cancel the whole thing. I need time to get my head straight. Time away from *her*. Instead, she will be sitting beside me tonight, a beautiful thorn in my side that's impossible to ignore.

I should have left her at the hotel. But that wasn't an option. I need her at my side. I'm the big picture guy. I sell clients on the broad strokes of my plans. Jade knows the numbers. The details. If a client has a specific question, she's usually the one to talk to. Her presence is invaluable. She seems cool and collected now, unlike me. My great hope is that she can keep the meeting on track.

We get to the restaurant, and they seat us immediately.

We're a few minutes early. Enough time to appear courteous, but not so much that we look desperate. The potential clients arrive shortly after. Four Japanese businessmen. They speak perfect English. All of them have been to American colleges before returning to Japan. I've done my research on them before coming here.

We start with some small talk and a few drinks to loosen everyone up. This part is easy. All I do is ask a lot of questions. It makes the client feel like I'm interested. I *am* interested, but this is how I communicate that to them.

The hard part is deciding when to start to sell. I don't want to rush it, but I don't want to take too long either. Normally, I have a natural feel for when it's time to strike, but not tonight. I'm trying to listen to the client, but all I can think about is Jade sitting next to me.

She sits so close to me her thigh is almost touching mine. Once she moved and her flesh felt soft against mine. Her hand brushes my sleeve and I fucking get hard. Christ, I have it so bad for her. I shift slightly to hide my growing arousal beneath the table. I don't think Jade notices.

If she does, she's not showing signs of it.

If anything, she's more on her game tonight than I've ever seen her. Cool, confident, and fun. Before I know it, she's transitioning the conversation smoothly into our sales pitch.

I stare at her impressed.

She is different, and it's not just her looks. I realize that it *is* her appearance that brought about the change. She's not pretending to be something she's not tonight. This is her. The real her. Now that she's not hiding behind her dumpy clothes, she's confident and sure of herself.

I like this new version of her. I wish I'd seen her like this before. It's a shame my hang ups about beautiful women forced her to hold back. Her initiative triggers something in me, and suddenly, I get into the groove, and focus on business again.

I don't stop her, though.

She's on a roll and it's beautiful to watch. The clients are eating out of her hand, and they're engaged with what she's saying. I jump into the conversation without interrupting her rhythm. For the first time, the sales pitch is an equal effort between Jade and me. We make a good team. We're picking up each other's ideas and running with them, almost like we'd rehearsed this. Except it feels completely natural.

Like we're in sync.

The clients are on board with what we offer them. They haven't agreed to anything yet, but I'm sure they will. They order us another round of drinks. I've already had too many sakes. I'm not drunk, but I'm close.

I need to keep my wits about me, not just because of the clients, but because of Jade. Things between us are getting complicated. Or, at least, they're getting complicated for me. I can't stop thinking about her as more than just my assistant tonight. I can't stop wanting her to *be* more than just my assistant. Any more alcohol and who knows what might happen?

I'm about to decline the next drink.

Jade tugs on my arm. Her eyes are glittering and her cheeks look flushed.

I've never seen her like this. It makes the blood in my veins sing. I lean in close to her. The smell of her perfume surrounds me. I inhale it like a drug. She smells like an exotic garden. For a second, I can't remember why I leaned in at all.

"You have to drink," she whispers.

"Are you trying to get me drunk?"

"No," she says quietly. "In their business culture, real conversations only occur when everybody is sloshed. The next morning all is forgotten on the surface, but the subtext and the friendship is not."

I shake my head and snap back to reality. "Right. Shit. I knew that. Thanks for the reminder."

This is the exactly the kind of distraction I don't need. I studied my prospects. I know the protocols. But I lost sight of that because I have other things on my mind tonight. Better things. Hotter things. I have to refocus. This deal is almost closed. I can't screw it up now.

When the next round of drinks came, we all lift our glasses and drink. My head is foggy. I hope this is the last one.

It isn't.

We stumble out of the restaurant. It's hot outside. It matches the inferno burning in my veins and the need pounding in my body.

Our Japanese clients are singing tunelessly. They can barely stand. They clap me on the back. We are all best friends now.

The deal is in the bag.

I try to help them into the back of the two black Mercedes Jade arranged for them, and almost fall in myself. They think that is hilarious and cannot stop laughing at Remington San.

Both Jade and I stand in the heat of the night and wave them off.

I feel Jade swaying next to me.

Our limo rolls up in front of us. I half-carry, half-push her into the backseat and go around to the other side. My entrance is not a graceful affair. My feet get twisted up and my ass lands hard on the seat.

Jade laughs. "You're drunk, Mr. Remington," she slurs.

I lean my head against the seat. "Yes, I am, Miss. Emerson, but so are you."

The car takes a corner and she falls against my side. A jolt shoots through me at the feel of her against me. I perk up a bit through my drunken haze. It's just her arm leaning against mine, but somehow it feels like the most intimate moment we've ever shared.

I raise the partition as we speed off into the night. I'm trying not to get swept up in the moment. I should just keep it professional.

"You did great tonight," I say. "You're the one who sealed that deal. Not me."

She leans her head on my shoulder, and suddenly, it's difficult to breathe. "You helped, a whole lot," she mumbles.

"Even so, I'm impressed."

She giggles. "I bet you say that to all your assistants."

I smile down indulgently at her. Inside the cool cocoon of this car, it feels as if she belongs to me. Warm feelings fill my chest. I'm not sure if it's her or the alcohol. Maybe both. "I really don't. You're the first assistant I've said that to."

She tilts her head up and our eyes meet. "Well, I'm honored, then, Sir," she says, staring into my eyes. Her cheeks are flushed, making her look even more beautiful. She nestles her head against my chest.

I worry she'll hear how fast my heart is beating. My arm is wedged between us and she shifts slight so her breast presses into me. She has no idea of the effect she has on me. She's just drunk and almost certainly jetlagged. My insides clench at the feeling of her soft flesh squashed against me. I move, trying to make some space, but when I do, she follows, pushing even closer to me now.

"Thank you for bringing me with you on this trip," she murmurs.

"No, need to thank me. I couldn't leave you behind. After how you handled yourself tonight, you'll be coming to all my meetings with me."

I feel her head nod against my chest. "Good. I'd like that. I've never been out of the country before. And certainly, never to a place like this." She tries to make a sweeping movement with her hand and it falls flat on my chest.

Her breath is warm against my skin. It sends tingling sensations radiating through my body. Desire rises up in me, hot and hard. The longer I spend this close to her, the more difficult it is to keep my thoughts clean.

"I haven't been this drunk since I was fifteen," she adds. "When I accidentally drank a whole load of spiked punch. It was horrible. Ugh. I threw up all over my dress. And it was new too." She hiccups. "Oh, ha-ha. I mean, what kind of spider is blue?" She looks at me with adoring eyes. "And you killed it. My hero."

The words are out of my mouth before I can stop them, "You're beautiful."

She gawks back at me, those sensuous hazel eyes wide with shock. "What?"

"You heard me." I reach down and stroke her chin.

"Do you want to hear a secret?"

"Sure."

"Pinky promise?"

I can't believe that I'm entangling my little finger with her. "Satisfied?"

She takes a deep breath and confesses, "I think you're really, really, really beautiful," she stage-whispers.

I smile and she catches my hand putting it in her lap. She lets go of my hand, but I don't pull it away from her. I let it rests high on her thigh. My fingertips caress her skin softly through the fabric of her dress. My touch is light. I'm not sure she can even feel it.

I know I shouldn't be touching her like this. This is crossing a line, but she feels so damn good. I trace light circles on the material of her dress.

Jade sighs in contentment and nestles closer to me.

My hand keeps moving in the same spot. Every swirl of my fingers pulls the hem of her dress higher. Her skin is pale in the darkness. My eyes savor every inch of flesh as more and more is revealed. My cock aches with excitement. I can't remember the last time I've been so turned on.

Jade's breathing quickens. I feel it in the steady rise and fall of her chest against my arm. It makes me bolder. I slide her dress up more, to the point where I can almost see the cleft between her legs. My hand is on her skin now, with nothing separating us.

She moans softly against me. Her hips are shifting now, almost imperceptibly, but the movement is hiking her dress up farther, revealing the white lace of her panties. My whole body throbs with desire. My cock strains against my zipper, begging for release.

I slip my hand between her thighs and run my finger over

her panties. She's soaking wet. She moans again. The sound sends shivers through me and urges me on.

My fingers slide over her in a steady rhythm. Her sweet juices slick my fingers, making it feel like nothing at all is separating me from her. Jade grabs my wrist, and I think she's going to stop me. Instead, she pulls my hand against her. Her hips push up.

She wants more.

I slide my hand into her panties. She's blazing hot beneath my touch. My fingers part her silky folds and I plunge a digit into her wetness. She gasps and clenches around me, tight and eager. I rest my palm over her hard clit while I stroke her.

Jade buries her face in my chest to muffle the moans and little breathless sounds that escape her throat. I stroke her hair with one hand while I work the other furiously between her thighs. She squirms and rubs herself desperately against my hand. I speed up in response. I want to push her to her limits and beyond.

Her cries are louder now. I can tell by the way her body is squirming that she can't hold back any longer. Her whole body tenses up against me in sweet release.

When she can breathe again, I tilt her head up to look at her. Our eyes meet, and I see my own desire reflected back at me. "You're so fucking beautiful," I say.

Just then, the limo stops. I look out the window to see our hotel.

We can't get upstairs fast enough.

CHAPTER 5

JADE

Luke pulls me into the suite, and I'm tearing his clothes off before he can even close the door. What he did to me in the limo was amazing, but I need more. A lot more.

His jacket comes off first. I run my fingers over his chest, savoring the feeling of him. Then I yank his shirt open, scattering buttons all over the room. This isn't the first time I'm seeing his chest, but it's the first time I can touch it.

His muscles tense where my fingers graze his skin. Power radiates from him. It's as if that winged dragon tattoo is vibrating beneath my palms. I shiver at the feeling. It's one thing to see how strong he is. It's another to feel it up close.

He shrugs his shirt from his shoulders, and it falls to the floor. My hands trail down his hard stomach, like I want to memorize every inch of him. Hungrily, I unfasten his belt and unbutton his pants.

Luke watches me, his eyes hooded and glazed with lust. For two months, I've wanted Luke from afar, hated every woman who went out on his arm, or made the tabloid covers. Now he is here with *me* making my nerves sizzle as if they're on fire.

I pull his zipper down and feel his hardness thrusting at the material as I do it. His pants fall away, and I'm back where I was a few hours ago, him standing in front of me in just his underwear. There's no mistaking the thick length of him straining against his boxer briefs.

I stroke the length of it. It quivers beneath my hand, alive and eager. He groans. The sound is low and deep. It resonates inside me, filling me with desire.

I can barely believe this is happening. This had just been a wild fantasy. Now it is coming true. I shoot Luke a look as I tug his underwear down his hips. His face looks strained with raw hunger. Then his cock is springing up in front of my face, begging for me.

I run my tongue along his shaft. He tastes salty and manly. Luke grunts. I like hearing the animal-like noise coming from his mouth. It lets me know I'm making him feel good. Like I'm sexy and desirable. It urges me on.

I take his thick head between my lips, and my tongue swirls around him, tracing his ridges. I glance up. His eyes are closed, and he is breathing heavily. I enjoy seeing him like this, under my control for once.

As if he reads my thoughts, he reaches down, grabbing my arms, and raises me up. "If you keep doing that, sugar, I'm gonna explode, and I'm not ready to do that." He takes a step back from me. "Strip for me. I want to see everything I didn't see this afternoon."

I unzip my dress and let it slide off me. I reach behind and unclasp my bra. It springs away, and I shimmy out of it, deliberately making my breast jiggle.

"Oh fuck," he groans thickly.

I slip my fingers into the rim of my panties and slip it down my thighs. My movements are still unsteady with the alcohol buzzing in my veins, and I nearly trip and fall over.

He catches my almost naked body and lifts me into his strong arms.

"Oh wow," I say breathily, staring up at him in wonder.

He carries me to his bedroom and drops me unceremonious onto his bed. I look up at him with wide eyes as he tears my panties from my hips with a single movement and tosses them to the floor.

"Spread your legs," he orders.

I obey and he stands over me, his eyes roving, taking in all of me, then stopping between my legs. Normally, this kind of intense scrutiny would make me feel self-conscious, but tonight I'm too drunk to care. Besides, I can see how turned on he's getting just from looking at me. He's literarily licking his lips at the sight of my bare pussy.

"You're all mine, Jade," he says, almost growling. "I'm gonna make you come harder than you've ever come before."

"No one's stopping you," I say daringly.

Instantly, he's beside me. His thick length digging against my thigh, hot and hard, his breath smelling of the mango we had for desert and sake.

My head is swimming, but I want to kiss him so badly. I crave to know what that sweet fruit will feel like on my tongue when filtered through the sexiest man I've ever met. His mouth swoops down on mine, warm and demanding. His tongue pushes in, and I moan into him. As I suck his tongue and lose myself in that kiss, my body melts into his, and I forget where he ends and I begin.

Time passes. Minutes, maybe hours pass.

Then Luke raises his head and gazes down at me. His eyes burn into mine, then he dives in, licking, sucking, and biting my nipples. First one, then the other. I run my fingers through his hair and pull him closer to me. He trails kisses down my neck and chest nipping at my heated flesh. It sends jolts of pleasure straight to my core.

I feel like I'm floating now, like if Luke wasn't on top of me, I would drift up to the ceiling. Pleasure rocks through me. His mouth is electric. It sends my passion soaring to dizzying heights. I feel like I'm about to lose my mind.

His hand slides down my body to rest between my legs. He circles my clit, reigniting that fire that he started in the limo. My insides throb with an empty ache, needing to be filled. My hips push impatiently against his hand.

Suddenly, Luke grabs me and flips me over. My body presses against him, skin on skin. I love the way it feels, like I could touch every part of him at once.

His big hands run possessively over my body. Without warning, he claws his hand into my hair, and yanks my head back so my throat is pulled up and exposed to him. "I want to feel the need beating in your blood," he snarls, seconds before I feel his teeth bite down on my neck, and his thick finger pushes into me.

I cry out with pain and pleasure. His mouth sucks at the pulse at my neck while he adds another finger inside me. They slide in and out of me, teasing me. I grind my hips against his hand, wanting more. It feels so damn good, but this isn't enough. My body demands more. "I need you, Luke," I groan.

"Do you?"

"I need you so bad."

"Do you want me to fuck you?"

His words send a shiver through me. "Yes."

"Say it," he says, his voice thick with desire. "Tell me what you want."

"I want you to fuck me," I beg. The desperation in my voice matches the naked need inside me.

As soon as the words are out of my mouth, Luke rolls me roughly onto my back. He grabs my ankles and hauls my ass to the edge of the mattress. He leans over me with his arms on either side of me, and positions his ready cock between my legs, not entering me just resting against my lips.

My body trembles with anticipation.

"Yeah, I can fuck you," he growls as he slams into the very depths of me.

My whole body jerks with the power of his thrust. He feels so big and amazing inside me. I've wanted this for so long. I had no idea how badly I needed this. How badly I need him.

He rocks his hips, sliding in and out of me. Every stroke of his cock elicits a moan from me. I can't stop myself. He's in total control of me. I never want him to stop. I grab his hips to urge him on.

Luke watches my face as he rams into me. He's not thinking of someone else or something else. Right this moment, I am his whole world. There is nothing else except his cock deep inside my pussy. He leans down to kiss me. It sends a potent wave through me.

Luke moves faster now. His breathing is ragged. It's punctuated by grunts of pleasure. He's so powerful and primal. He's finding the most sensitive parts of me, building that delicious pressure up inside me. All I can do is hold onto him and let him pleasure me like I've never been pleasured before.

Every pound pushes me closer to the breaking point. My hips buck beneath him, in time with his thrusts, burying him as deep inside me as he can go. Every nerve ending inside me screams at the feeling.

Pleasure rushes through me, hot and wild. There's no stopping it. No holding back. My entire body clenches in ecstasy as my orgasm rips through me. Luke roars above me, then freezes, as his cock spasms inside me, and fills me with his hot cum. We come together, joined in the most intimate way possible. Everything else in the world ceases to exist except the two of us, locked in pleasure.

A long time later, he slides out of me and lays on the bed. His hands pull me next to him, and he wraps his arm around me.

I lean my head against his chest. The sound of his heartbeat matches my own. "That was amazing."

"You are amazing," he says, holding me close.

Almost immediately, exhaustion overwhelms me. My eyes drift close, and I'm asleep.

CHAPTER 6

JADE

I pry my eyelids open and flinch in the glaring morning light. Yellow sunlight is streaming in through the windows. My head pounds, and my mouth is dry and sour. The slight movement makes my head throb even worse.

How much did I have to drink last night?

I'm not a heavy drinker. A few glasses of wine to take the edge off after work was about as tipsy as I ever get. I don't have time to go out and party like I did in college. Luke keeps me too busy for that.

Luke. Fuck.

I swivel my head slowly, trying not to piss off the giant hammering away on the inside of my skull.

Luke lies next to me. He's not wearing any clothes.

Neither am I.

Holy shit.

The events of last night are hazy. Once the drinks started

flowing, everything after is foggy. Like something from a half-remembered dream. But it wasn't a dream. Waking up naked in Luke's bed is proof enough that what happened last night was very real.

Oh, shit. We didn't even use a condom!

I inch my way off the bed, slowly and quietly. I can't wake him up. I don't want him to see me like this. It was fine last night, I was tanked up on alcohol and lust, but I can't handle it in the harsh light of day. Worse, I might see regret in his eyes. I definitely couldn't handle that right now. My head hurts too much to even think rationally.

I need to get away.

The world spins when I stand up. I freeze and wait for my head to clear. There's a good chance I'm still drunk, but not in a fun way. Painfully, I locate the first of my discarded clothes. The tattered remnants of my torn panties. The image of Luke tearing them from my hips and flinging them away flashes in my head.

Fuck, that was hot.

I tiptoe out his bedroom into the living area. Gathering my clothes to my chest, I make to my bedroom, and I shut the door behind me quietly. For the first time since I woke up, I feel like I can actually breathe.

I walk to the minibar thinking about what happened last night. I wanted it to happen. I've wanted it for so long, but now I kinda regret it. Last night was a mistake. A beautiful, orgasmic mistake. Luke and I have crossed a line, one I'm not sure we can come back from. Things between us will change, and I can't be sure it would be a change for the better.

I grab a bottle of water from the fridge, rip the cap off, and down it in one long gulp. It tastes better than anything I've ever had in my life. I can almost feel the hydration spread through my parched body. It's a step in the right direction.

My head still hurts, though, and my eyes still feel sandy. I need something else. Sugar. I search the mini bar and find a bottle of some brown liquid. The writing on the label is in a language I can't read, but I'm not going to let that stop me. I take a long swig from the bottle. It's creamy and chocolatey, and I perk up a bit, starting to feel human again. Thank God for caffeine.

The whole point of his rule about not hiring attractive women to work for him is that they are too much of a distraction for him. What would he think about me now? If just being around a pretty girl was too much for him, how would he handle a woman he'd slept with? I sit on the bed with a groan. Last night is looking more and more like a terrible mistake.

My brain is too muddled to think this through. I need someone to talk to, someone who isn't half-dead with a hangover. I fish my phone from my purse and call Emma.

She answers on the third ring, "Bitch, do you know what time it is over here?"

Her voice is loud, but it's still good to hear it. "Yeah," I say. "It's like nine o'clock at night over there."

She laughs. "Damn. I was trying to mess with you. But of course, you know the time difference, you nerd."

"You'll have to try harder than that." I smile weakly. This is why I love her. She can always make me laugh with her cheerful chat, no matter how bad I'm feeling.

"Yeah, yeah. So how's the trip? You better be taking lots of pictures to show me when you get back."

"Things would be better if I wasn't so frigging hungover," I say.

"Well, well," Emma says. "Look at you going wild now that you're out of the country. I've been begging you to come out with me for months."

"Yeah, well, if you took me somewhere like Bangkok, I'd go."

Emma laughs. "Bangkok. Have you banged any cock yet?"

I groan at the joke. Not just because it's cheesy, but because it hits too close to home. "Now that you mention it."

"Shut the fuck up!" She screams. "You're kidding me? You got laid?"

"I did."

"I don't believe it," she says firmly.

"Well, it's the truth."

She laughs. "Who's the lucky guy? Was it a local? Some swarthy Thai fisherman with really rough hands? Ooh, or a sweaty kick boxer?"

"No, to all of those," I say with a sigh. "Are those the type of guys you think I'm in to?"

"I don't know *what* you're in to. Before you left, I would have said you're into celibacy and lonely masturbation."

"Ass," I reply, but I can't suppress a smile. She isn't totally wrong.

Emma continues right along, "But apparently, Bangkok Jade likes to get freaky. Good for you."

I shake my head, even though she can't see me. "I don't know if it's a good thing."

"Why not? It's about time someone knocked the cobwebs off that pussy."

I laugh. "You're terrible."

"Ehh, I'm just happy for you. So why aren't you? Happy, I mean."

"Because I slept with my boss."

There's a pause on the other end, then an explosion, "You're shitting me! You and Luke-mother effing-Remington? The richest, hottest man in New York? Fuck me, I'm impressed."

"Don't be," I mutter glumly. "I'm pretty sure it was a huge mistake."

She laughs. "How huge are we talking? Like eight inches? *Nine?*" She pauses, then asks incredulously, "Ten?"

"Stop it, Emma. I'm serious. He's my boss. I don't know what's going to happen between us now."

"It'll be fine," she says. "It's not like you got him drunk and had your way with him."

"He *was* pretty drunk."

"You seduced him. You sly, little minx," Emma says, giggling maniacally. "I didn't think you had it in you."

53

"Hang on. I was drunk, too," I protest. "We both were."

"Well, tell me everything, then."

"We met with some clients, and things got a bit out of hand in the back of the limo. We ended up back in his room, and well…"

"He pounded you like a stubborn nail?"

I ignore her comment. "But now I don't know what to do when I see him again. I feel like it's going to be awkward."

"It shouldn't be. Unless *you* make it awkward."

"What does that mean?" I ask.

"Look, you're two consenting adults. You're both single. There's nothing wrong with having a little fun. I mean, you *did* have fun, right?"

"I did."

"And I'm sure he had fun with Sexy Jade," she says. "So the best thing you can do is see how he reacts when he sees you and just play along. Then, it won't be weird."

"What if he fires me?" I ask, finally giving voice to my biggest fear.

"Then he's an idiot and you sue his ass for wrongful termination."

"I could never do that," I argue.

"Well, whatever," Emma says. "My point is that he'd be dumb to fire you after sleeping with you. So he'll probably react one of a few ways. He might pretend it never happened, in which case, you pretend the same thing. He might acknowledge it and say it'll never happen again. Or he'll want to keep plowing your bean field. Then, it's up to you what you want to do."

"The problem is I don't know *what* I want to do."

"Liar," Emma taunts.

I sigh with frustration. "How did I get myself into this mess?"

Emma laughs. "Well, when a boy has a rocking body and a cute butt, and a girl has worn her vibrator down to a nub, sometimes—"

"Okay," I say, cutting her off. "I get it. I have to go."

"Good luck out there," she quips.

"Thanks. I'm gonna need it."

CHAPTER 7

JADE

I sit in the restaurant and stare at the plate of breakfast in front of me. I don't even know why I heaped all this food onto my plate from the buffet. My stomach is still churning uneasily. Looks like I have to pass on the eggs and bacon, but the toast is probably safe. Maybe it can soak up some of the alcohol. Although I probably need to eat a whole loaf's worth of bread to do that.

The moment I take a bite, Luke lowers himself into the seat across from me. The sight of him does nothing to calm my queasy stomach. His hair is wet from his shower, and instead of looking rough, he looks drop-dead gorgeous. My mouth goes dry, making it difficult to chew the toast. His expression is unreadable and I feel my cheeks flush with warmth.

"Good morning, Jade."

"Morning," I mutter, feeling extremely self-conscious. I force myself to look at him calmly. I knew I'd have to see him again today, but I hoped to delay it until I felt more like myself. But the dreaded confrontation is happening now. There's no getting around it. No getting around *him*. I might as well face him now and find out what the fallout from our drunken tryst would be.

Overwhelmed by his smoldering blue eyes, I swallow my toast and nearly choke. I gulp down some coffee. Last night hasn't changed anything for me. I still find him incredibly hot, maybe even more so. No matter what happened before or what would happen in the future, he's still the sexiest freaking man I've ever seen. I take a gulp of coffee.

He speaks first, "About last night—"

I swallow the coffee in a rush and interrupt him. I have to. I'm too nervous about what he will say. Afraid he will say he wants me gone. "Luke, stop. It's okay, you don't have to worry. I just want to forget about last night. We were both very drunk. I can barely remember what we did, anyway. Can we just pretend it never happened? Is that okay?"

Luke gazes at me, confident and unashamed. "Is that what you want?"

I can't tell whether he's upset or relieved so I plough on, "Yes. It's what I want."

"Too bad," he says firmly.

His answer startles me. "What?"

"I can't pretend it never happened," he says. "And I don't want to forget about it." He leans forward intently and pins me with his sapphire eyes. "It's all I've been thinking about since I woke up this morning. It's a shame you were already gone."

I shake my head. "You don't think it was a mistake?"

"The only mistake I made was not seeing how beautiful you are sooner."

My breath catches in my throat. Does he really mean it? I find it hard to believe. Maybe he's just trying to smooth things over with me. He regrets what happened, but doesn't want things to be awkward between us.

I imagine that as soon as we land in America, he'll distance himself from me. Maybe I'll get transferred to another department in the company. Maybe he'll fire me. I need to fix this myself before things get out of hand. "Listen, Luke," I say. "We were drunk. We didn't know what we were doing."

"I was drunk, yes. But the most intoxicating thing last night was the touch of your lips on mine."

Holy shit.

Warmth floods my body, and butterflies take flight in my stomach. I'm dizzy. My whole world is spinning.

"I knew exactly what I was doing last night," he says. "And I know exactly what I want to do to you again. I know you want it, too."

I open my mouth to deny it, but the words don't come. He's right. I desperately want him. I could quite easily let him take me right now. But I'm afraid. He awakens feelings inside of me that I can't control. It's thrilling and terrifying, all at the same time.

That's Luke Remington in a nutshell.

The very thing that makes him so sexy is the same thing that makes him so intimidating. He's sexy and powerful, dominant and cocky, unstoppable and irresistible. He's like a force of nature, sweeping me up in his strength. I feel powerless against him. Still, I have to try and resist. "Luke," I say, shaking my head. "I think you were right all along. We shouldn't have mixed business and pleasure. I don't know if I can be as professional as I was while we are sleeping together. I'm worried that I'll screw up and disappoint you. If we put this little hiccup behind us now, maybe then things will to go back to normal between us."

He laughs humorlessly. "What you call normal between us was based on a lie. *Your* lie."

My eyes widen. "I don't understand."

"The day you showed up in my life wearing a costume, you lied about who you are."

I shake my head. "It wasn't a costume. And my appearance has nothing to do with who I am. I'm still the same woman you hired."

His eyes become stormy. "That's where you're wrong. Your appearance has everything to do with who you are."

I lean back in my chair and stare at him, disappointed. I can't believe he could be such a shallow egoist. "Oh, so just because you now think I'm attractive, that somehow changes who I am inside?"

Luke slams his hand on the table, making me jump. "Dammit, Jade. You're smarter than this. *You* changed who you are inside by changing your appearance. I saw you last night with our clients. You weren't the meek and mousy Jade you've been pretending to be. You were sparkling. Those guys were eating from the palm of your hand. That was the real you. The normal you. And that was all because of how you looked. You weren't hiding behind your dumpy facade. Surely, you noticed the difference inside yourself?"

I hadn't considered that. I forgot the client meeting while being in the complicated situation I found myself in this morning. Between the hangover and the wild sex with my boss, I barely remembered how I'd acted with the clients. Now that Luke has called it to my attention, I know he's right.

I had been on my game last night. At points, it felt like I ran the whole meeting, even though Luke sat beside me. He contributed to the conversation, but I'd been in control. No other client meeting had gone like that. I usually sit back and let Luke work his magic. But not last night. Last night, I felt confident, and let myself shine. It never occurred to me it might have something to do with the way I was dressed, but it certainly made sense.

"You know I'm right," Luke says.

"So what if you are?"

"So that means last night was the real you. Everything before that was a lie. If you want things to be normal between us, then you need to be the Jade from last night. Not the fake Jade you've been for the last two months."

My head pounds away. "And you want the version of me who sleeps with you?"

He shoots me a cocky grin. "Damn right I do. And not just because you've never been sexier, but because the new version of you is a force to be reckoned with. With you at my side, we can take over the whole fucking world."

As much as I like the sound of that, I'm scared, too. I have to ask him the question burning inside me, "Has sleeping with you become part of my job description now?"

He frowns. "Of course not. It's not a job requirement. You don't have to sleep with me. Only if you want to, but I know you do." Luke leans in close to me so no one else can hear. "In fact, if it wasn't for this damn conference, I'd take you upstairs right now and fuck you senseless."

My heart stops beating in my chest. I can't breathe. Wetness pools between my legs. He's right. Since the day I started working for Luke, I've imagined what it would be like to be with him. Idle day dreams turned to sultry fantasies of feeling his strong hands all over my body. None of those fantasies can compare to the real thing. Now that I've gotten a taste of him, I need more. I would welcome him into my body anywhere, anytime he chooses to avail himself to me. In fact, my only objection would be to being drunk next time. I want all of my senses sharp, so I can savor the feelings he ignites in me.

"We didn't use a condom last night," he says softly. "Are you protected?"

I flush to the roots of my hair. "Yes, I'm on the pill," I admit, then I hurry to add, "but I've never gone bare before."

He flashes his teeth. "Neither have I. My mother was such a proponent of safe sex I'm sure she would have preferred me to jerk off into a condom too."

I giggle and he laughs too. For a while, there is no tension between us. Then that sexual thing rears its head again. My head is still throbbing and all I want is to be back in bed with him.

"I should go," I say.

"You haven't eaten your breakfast yet."

I shrug. "Nah. My stomach feels funny."

"Then wait for me, and we'll attend the seminar together."

"Uh, I'm not attending the morning sessions. I have to go up and prepare the sheets for your talk this afternoon."

He frowns. "When will I see you again?"

"Mr. Dimitriou is just going to brief you, so you won't need me for that. I'll see you for lunch with Carl at the Golden Orchid restaurant. It's on the third floor."

"Fine. I better go get some food then," he says standing up. Before I can do anything, he bends down and brushes his lips against mine. As if we are a couple. As if that is the most natural thing in the world for him to do. I watch his tall imposing figure stride away, my heart hammering in my chest.

CHAPTER 8

JADE

Upstairs in the printing room, I meet another one of the speaker's PA. A sweet local woman called Anong. She too, is preparing hard copies of the presentation to be handed to the attendees of her boss's talk. She hands me a green and white box. It says Tiffy on the outside and is written in English on one site. It's a Thai version of Acetominophen. They are very effective and in less than twenty minutes, my headache is gone. I tell her that I need to pop down to the hotel's boutique to buy a suit for a lunch meeting.

"No. No," she says shaking her hand. "Hotel boutique very expensive. Come with me I show you very good shop," she offers.

I look at her doubtfully. "How far away is it?"

"Next door. You will like." She nods vigorously.

I grin at her. "Okay."

The shop turns out to be the gift that keeps on giving. It is one of those amazing little places that sells knock-off designer gear for one tenth of the price in other shops. I have heard of these secret places where you could go and get tailored suits for fifty American dollars. Like a kid in a sweet shop, I buy dresses, pant-suits, skirts, tops, jackets, shoes, bags and scarves. In less than an hour, I max out both my credit cards and leave carrying six bags of stuff for me. I even got a gorgeous silk suit for Emma. It's one of those classic #sorrynotsorry moments. I've blown six months of wages, but heck, I won't have to shop for the next five years!

After running up to my room to change, I come down in a fitted red suit to meet Luke and Carl Magnus for lunch at the Golden Orchid. I'm ten minutes early, so I walk into the restaurant, hoping that the men aren't here yet. I want a few minutes to compose myself. Get a handle on whatever is happening between us. Things are quickly spiraling out of control with Luke. It's not necessarily a bad thing, but this isn't who I am. I never leap before I look. I need something to clutch to right now, when my whole damn world feels like it's been turned upside down.

But of course, both Luke and Carl Magnus are already at the table.

Carl is one of our major Swedish clients. Though I've never met him in person before, I've spoken to him on the phone a few times and I've seen pictures of him before. They don't do him justice. He's a hellva lot better looking in person.

His Viking heritage is clear. He's a big man, about the size of Luke, but with broader shoulders. Long blond hair frames his rugged face. Despite the tailored suit he's wearing, he looks about two seconds from tearing his clothes off and charging into battle.

I perceive all this in a distant way, because even though he's startlingly handsome with beautiful grass-green eyes, he's just not my type. And even if he were, my heart doesn't have room in it for anyone else but Luke. I've spent the last two months falling for my boss, and the last twenty-four hours have been the culmination of all those feelings.

Luke notices me first. His blue eyes shine at me like a beacon, dimming everything else in the dining room. I can't look away from him. His eyes devour me. Then he smiles and his crooked smile makes my heart flutter.

Like a proper gentlemen, both men stand as I approach.

Carl's eyes move appreciatively over my body. "Miss Jade Emerson. In the flesh," he says softly. His voice is deep, warm and accented.

I smile politely. "Mr. Magnus."

I reach out my hand for a handshake, but he ignores it and sweeps me into a hug. The unexpected familiarity, so unlike the exceptionally polite and distant way the Japanese clients greeted me last night, startles me, but Carl is an important client.

"I can't breathe," I say breathlessly.

Carl laughs and puts me down. Then he kisses me on one cheek, and then the other. It's an oddly delicate greeting after the bear hug, but he's European. I assume it's how they do things over there.

"My apologies, Jade," he says. "Can I call you, Jade?"

My eyes widen. "Yes, of course."

"Good. You must call me Carl."

"Okay."

"It's just nice to put such a beautiful face to the efficient voice on the phone."

I blush at that, not expecting the compliment. Again, he's being a bit forward, but I don't call him on it, out of politeness. Besides, that may be the way they do things in Sweden. Anyway, he hasn't really crossed any lines. Luke would certainly step in if he had done that. I glance at him, but he just stands there, flashing me his billion-dollar smile, so everything must be okay.

Both men wait until I sit down before taking their own seats. It's just the three of us at the table, so I sit between Luke and Carl. I'm still reeling from Carl's exuberant greeting, but luckily, Luke is on his game. He jumps right into business discussions, allowing me to sit back for a moment and gather my bearings.

CHAPTER 9

LUKE

I'm talking business with Carl, but it's almost like my brain is on auto-pilot. The way he hugged and kissed Jade is still making my blood boil. It took all my willpower not to push the fucking table over and yank him off her.

Carl is a good client, but I have no problem punching him in his stupid, cocky face if he tries something like that again with her. As it is, I'm half tempted to cut this meeting short right now and sever all ties with him. There are other Swedish fish in the sea. I don't need him.

But I know that's just my temper getting the better of me, so I pretend as if nothing is wrong and smile.

Jade shoots me a worried glance, then she relaxes, and sits down.

I watch the curve of her smile as she takes the menu from the waitress. I stare at her. I still can't believe her complete transformation from dowdy librarian to this raving beauty sitting beside me.

I don't know when it happened exactly, but sometime yesterday, she became incredibly important to me. She went from being my assistant to being a woman I can't stop thinking about.

Something about her drives me wild in a way I've never felt.

There have been plenty of other women in my life, but they tended to be casual affairs. They come, literally, and then go. It's not a conscious decision on my part, and it's not their fault either. I just tire quickly. Most of the time it's like, I take them to bed, and by the morning, I already want nothing to do with them.

Maybe that makes me a womanizing bastard, but that's just how it was. I never lied to those women. They knew exactly what they were getting into when they hooked up with me. I gave them no illusions that it would be anything more than great sex. Some of them tried really hard to tantalize me. I've seen every trick in the book. They probably fooled themselves into believing that they were more special than the other women I'd run with, that they were the one who would finally tame me and make me theirs for good.

But they never were.

Then there's what-a-surprise, frumpy, dumpy' Jade. We've already had our night together. Really, I should be done with her, or at the very least, have started the distancing process, but I only want her even more. Now that I've seen the swan hiding underneath the ugly duckling clothing, I can't stop thinking of her. How good her body felt beneath mine, how sweet her pussy tasted, and how mesmerizing her face looks when I make her come. In the limo, and in my bed.

She is perfect for me.

It's a lot more than just how sexy she is. I actually like spending time with her that doesn't include sex. That's a massive difference from all the other women I usually hang with. I have no idea what makes Jade so special. All I know is that she is. She actually makes me happy, for fuck's sake.

The only fly in the ointment is that she's my assistant.

Dating my assistant feels crude and low-class. Only scum-bags do that. I can't exactly fire her, then ask her out on a date. I'm a bastard, but I'm not a fucking bastard. But I can't stop this freight train of desire either. I don't want to stop it. I don't want to throw her away like I've done with all the other women. I want to keep exploring her, both her body and her mind. I want to see where this goes.

The sound of Jade's laughter cuts through my train of thought. I had retreated into my own head while Carl kept talking, but now, I notice that he's sitting a lot closer to her than I like.

"You've never been to Sweden?" he says. "Well, that is some-thing we must fix very soon. I will show you all the wonderful things about my country, yes? I will fly you out there on my private jet and you will stay with me."

Jade smiles at him. "That sounds nice. I'm sure your country is beautiful."

"It will be even more beautiful with you in it," the smarmy bastard oozes.

Jade laughs.

My heart blazes with black fury.

"You're too kind, Carl," she says. "Maybe one day we can

arrange something, and I can visit. But you know how busy I am." She throws a look at me. "With Luke."

Carl has the balls to turn to me like we're fucking friends. "Luke, you can spare Jade for a week or two, can't you?"

I'm one second away from punching him in his smug fucking face, but I remind myself that I'm not in the jungle. I'm not a caveman. I'm not going to act impulsively. There is a better way. I smile. If he can't see it's a tiger's smile then he's a bigger fool than I think he is. "No, Carl, I actually can't spare her."

He doesn't even seem to notice the rage flaring inside me. Incredible!

Jade, who is obviously, a lot smarter than him, does. She turns and gazes at me with a worried expression.

"Don't be silly," Carl scoffs with a laugh. "Let her off the leash for—"

I slam my hand on the table, shaking the plates and the glasses. "Jade is not a fucking dog on a leash."

Half of the people in the restaurant stop talking and look in our direction. Jade blinks in confusion while Carl leans back slightly and regards me with a curious, almost satisfied expression.

I force myself to smile. I doubt it reaches my eyes, but it's the best I can do. "You're being inappropriate, Carl," I state, my voice tighter than I want it to be. "This is a business lunch. Act like a fucking professional and stop harassing my assistant."

The smile drops from his face. He looks from me to Jade and

back to me. "My apologies if I have offended you, Luke. Or you, Jade. I was just having a bit of fun."

"Well, don't," I snap. "If you want me to keep working with you, you'll go have your fun somewhere else."

Carl nods. "Yes, of course, Luke. You're right. That was unprofessional of me. I value your company's services. Sometimes my sense of humor doesn't translate to English."

I nod, giving him a graceful way to back down. I know damn well his English is perfect. It's his goddamn manners that are the problem, but I don't want things to escalate further than they already have.

"Well," Carl says, standing up. "I'm sorry for my rudeness, but I have another meeting to attend. Please excuse me." He nods and leaves without saying another word.

Jade watches him go, her mouth agape. When he disappears from sight, she whips her head around to face me. "He's our best European client. Why did you do that? We could have lost him."

I stare into her eyes, letting her feel the weight of my gaze. "Fuck him and his fucking business. He can walk if wants to. I'll replace him in no time."

"But—?"

"Jade Emerson, you belong to me and no one else. Is that understood?"

Her head jerks back and she gawks at me as if she can't believe her eyes. "What do you mean?"

I lean in. "I mean, if you want to be with me, then you are mine and only mine. You're a beautiful woman, Jade. Other men will always notice. But when they come around, I expect you to brush them off real quick."

"I wasn't flirting with him, if that's what you think," she gasps defensively.

"No, if I thought you were flirting with him, I wouldn't be sitting here with you right now. That would have been unacceptable." I pause and let that sink in. "But I'm just making this clear to you. I don't like games. I don't find it attractive to see other men fawn over you. If we're going to be together, it's just you and me. Nobody else."

She stares at me, silent.

"Now, I'll have to punish you for what you did."

CHAPTER 10

JADE

Luke signs for the bill and stands up. "Come, Jade," he growls.

Hell, I almost do, just from the completely authoritative sound of his voice. We walk together out of the restaurant. There is not a word exchanged all the way to the auditorium. We step into the darkened auditorium, and I can feel Luke's emotions pulsing off him in waves. I don't dare look up at him because his face seems like a stone mask.

A man with steel rim glasses is on the stage discussing the developing Asian markets. Dr. Marty Rambul is a titan in our field, and I've really wanted to hear this particular lecture ever since Luke told me about the conference. At any other time, I would have found this topic, and the accompanying slideshow, absolutely fascinating, but right now, all I can think of is Luke telling me I need to be punished.

Just the thought of it has lit a raging fire inside me. Luke heads to some seats right at the back of the room. We sit next to each other and I can't focus on anything else, but his hard body next to me. He appears to be entirely absorbed in what the speaker is saying, so I keep shooting glances at him. He is heart-stopping gorgeous in the dim light. Dark shadows accentuate his sharp cheekbones and his powerful jaw. I look at his ripe lips and remember how they felt on mine the night before. How I got lost inside him. The memory thrills me and makes me crave the real thing again. I wish he would kiss me.

He's sitting so close to me. One shift of my body and we'll be touching. I don't dare act on that impulse. We're in a room full of people. Even though we are sitting in the back row with no one directly around us, I'm not so brave that I can pounce on him in public. No matter how much I want to feel his lips on mine.

Luke looks at me, and my lips part. I desperately try to beam my urge into his brain. Wow, he must have read my thoughts in my eyes, or my body language, because he leans his face close to mine, and I move my face closer to receive the kiss.

Only he doesn't kiss me. He buries his head in my hair and growls softly into my ear, "Take off your panties, Jade."

His demand startles me. He can't be serious. I stare at him, and his eyes glint with something, something dark. And a blazing hunger for me.

"I can't do that," I whisper fiercely.

He leans in again. His warm breath tickles my ear, sending warmth fluttering through me. "You can, and you will," he says so firmly there is no room for argument. His tongue flicks out and licks my ear lobe.

I melt at the feeling.

It's a crazy request, but there's no harm in playing this game with him. It must turn him on to think I'm bare under my skirt. It's not like anyone will notice that I'm not wearing underwear. I've never gone commando, but the idea exhilarates me. "Okay," I say softly and I get up to go to the ladies' room.

Luke grips my wrist and pulls me down into my seat. "No," he commands. "Do it now. Right here."

Fear spikes my chest. I look around the room, where a few hundred people are sitting. Nobody is sitting in the back row with us, but any of these people could turn around and see me at any time. Someone could get up and leave the room. The guy giving the presentation might be able to see me.

"What if someone sees me," I hiss.

Luke grins wolfishly. "Then you better be careful."

I glance around the room again, trying to gauge my chances of getting caught. No one would really notice me back here, but all it would take is for someone to stand up and walk back here. Then I'd be caught with my pants down, literally.

The very idea scares me a little, but I realize I'm also astonishingly turned on and excited by the thought. There's something so incredibly naughty and erotic about exposing myself to him in public. Then again, maybe it's Luke's eyes roving over my body with a heated anticipation that's egging me on. Or maybe it's the stern expression on his face. There is no doubt in my mind that this is my punishment.

All I know is I'm going to do it.

I lift my skirt up to my thighs. Luke stares at my revealed flesh like he wants to devour it. The way he looks at me makes me feel sexy. It keeps me going. I look down and my skin seems almost to glow in the darkness. Too obvious. If anyone looks my way, they're going to notice immediately, but I take a deep breath and go for it.

I hike my skirt up to reveal my lacy red panties. Luke stares at them, and it's like a physical touch. He radiates excitement beside me, sending a thrill through me. I sit up subtly in the seat, lifting my ass. Hooking my fingers into my underwear, I slide them down.

Luke is breathing heavily now as he looks between my legs.

My heart hammers in my chest. I am exposed and vulnerable. My core clenches with arousal. This is so risky and insane, but damn it, if it isn't getting me so hot, I can barely stand it.

I slip my panties the rest of the way off and tug my skirt down to hide my nakedness. Then I look at Luke almost proudly. I'd met his challenge.

His eyes dance with desire. He takes the panties from my hand and lifts them up to his face. He inhales the scent of me deeply.

It's sexy as hell, but now anyone can turn around and see what he's doing. I yank his hand down to his lap to hide my panties from view.

He smiles seductively at me and stuffs my underwear into his jacket pocket, like he's claiming them as a prize.

I clench my thighs together to still the desperate ache there. Why the hell was this turning me on so much? If I don't find a way to calm down, I'm going to soak right through my skirt.

Luke leans back in his chair and turns his attention back to the speaker.

Confusion fills me. Was that it? Are we done? I follow his lead and settle into my seat as well. That's when I feel his hand on my thigh.

I keep my expression neutral, but inside, I'm in a frenzy of excitement. I should have known he wasn't finished with me.

His hand inches under the hem of my skirt until it is completely hidden. He caresses the sensitive skin on my inner thigh.

I want to stop him. If this keeps going, I have no idea how someone won't see us. But I'm too far gone. Desire takes ahold of me, and my sex burns with need. I let him keep going and just pray no one can see what's happening.

"Open," he whispers.

Dear God.

Luke's finger dips between my silky folds. I grit my teeth to keep the moan from escaping my throat. It comes out in a trembling breath instead. I look at Luke, my eyes wide, but he's looking straight ahead. Last night was hotter than anything that has ever happened to me, but this…this is a whole new level.

He continues to stroke me, and I grip the arms of my chair to steady myself. Each touch of his hand makes my hips want to squirm. I feel extra sensitive for some reason, maybe because of all the sex last night or because I know we shouldn't be doing this. It's dangerous and wrong, which strangely, just seems to heighten my senses.

Luke slicks his thumb in my juices and swirls it over my hard, throbbing clit.

It's like an electric shock jolts through me. I close my eyes. As much as I don't want to, I groan at the feeling. I try to cover the sound by turning it into a cough, but to me, it sounds utterly fake. No one turns around to look at me, though, which is good. I'm too wound up to feel relief.

The man talking on the podium in front of us practically vanishes from my consciousness as Luke lightly pinches my sensitive nub before his thumb plunges inside me. He forms a V with his fingers and slides it up either side, making me shift in my seat. How has no-one noticed us yet? I can only pray that we don't get thrown out before I climax.

He's moving with a steady, hypnotic rhythm. Every touch brings me closer and closer to the edge. I fight the feelings building inside me. I can't let myself go. If I do, there's no way I can keep quiet.

Pressure builds inside me like a volcano about to blow. Luke keeps caressing me, never letting up the delicious tempo. He's dragging me kicking and screaming over the edge. I can't stop him. I don't even want to stop him anymore. It feels too good. I barely care that I'm about to embarrass myself in front of an auditorium full of people. Rational thought is gone. I know I won't last anymore. I clench my teeth to keep from crying out.

"Look at me," he murmurs, his voice low but undoubtedly delivering an order.

My eyes flip open, and I meet his gaze. And that is it. No holding back. Pleasure erupts inside me, and I moan louder than I've ever moaned before.

At that exact moment, the entire room bursts into applause.

Jesus, are they clapping for me?

Through the haze of pleasure, I see the speaker on stage taking a bow. He just finished his lecture. They're clapping for him. No one heard the sound of my orgasm. Luke had timed my orgasm to finish with the speaker.

I curl up on my seat and let pleasure pulse through me. Luke's thumb is still inside me but no one is paying attention to me except Luke. He's the only one seeing me tremble uncontrollably. But he likes what he sees.

Finally, I slump back in my chair, satisfied and spent. Aftershocks of bliss pass through me, but the danger has passed. I'm free to savor the feelings rolling inside me. Luke catches the back of my head in one hand and lifts his other, the one that had, only a few moments ago, been in my pussy, to my lips. I open my mouth at once, and he slides his fingers past my lips. I massage them with my tongue, taking my time so I can taste myself on him, sucking lightly and watching as his brow furrow with arousal. That gives me an idea. It's a risky idea, but two can play at this game. I release his fingers.

Luke looks down at me, a crooked smile on his face. "So, what did you think?"

I laugh and shake my head. "Best Asian Development seminar ever."

CHAPTER 11

JADE

My panties are still in Luke's pocket, but I try to look as professional and decent as possible as we make our way backstage to get everything set up for Luke's presentation. He looks completely calm and in-control as he goes through his notes one last time, checking everything to make sure he has all his ideas in order.

"How are you not nervous?" I wonder aloud, watching as he straightens his tie and double-checks his prompts.

He shrugs. "I've done this a thousand times before, besides, my mind's on...other things." His eyes flick up and down my body, a small smile slipping onto his face.

I blush again. Because I want what he wants. Jesus, what kind of person do I turn into whenever this man is around? I perch on the edge of a desk off to the side of the stage, and try to think of some way to get rid of him for a minute. "Don't you need to go to the toilet first or something?"

"Good idea, I'll be back in two," he says, getting to his feet.

My heart is hammering as I watch him head off through a back door towards the toilets. Perfect-now is my time.

I glance around to make sure no-one is looking, then dive onto the stage. There are a few people who have chosen not to go for the break, but they seem to be busy looking through their notes, or chatting with the people sitting next to them. Nobody is looking at the empty stage.

I walk quickly and confidently across the stage towards the lectern. Luke's laptop is already on it. The lectern is covered by a heavy red velvet. I look around the hall once more. Everyone is busy doing their own thing.

Ducking down, I slip through the opening in the curtain around the lectern. As I guessed, the space underneath is wide enough to easily fit me if I maintain a squatting position. In fact, I can even get on my haunches. The curtain also completely covers me from view. I feel quite giddy. A part of me isn't really sure that I'm actually doing this. I raise myself up on my knees.

Yeah, this is an appropriate response to my punishment. Just like me, he'll have to come in a room full of people. Only, I didn't have to face them. But it'll be fine because the pool of light only falls on his face and his audience will mostly be looking at the sideshow. Besides, that look he gave me before he'd left for the toilet…he wants me to be daring.

I stay very still while someone introduces Luke.

A minute or two later, Luke walks out onto the stage to polite applause, and takes his place at the lectern. "Good afternoon, Ladies and Gentlemen," he greets them.

I reach up and run my hand over his package.

He looks down, eyes wide, but as soon as his gaze falls on me, he smiles. A secret smile. He wants this. He pretends to pull at something, while he tenderly tucks a strand of my hair behind my ear. He starts his presentation. I typed it up, so I know where the jokes are and the laughter and applause will be. I wait for it and take advantage of the noise to unzip his pants. He carries on talking as if nothing is happening. I reach into his boxers, and wrap my fingers around his erection. It is at full mast.

"Right, let's begin," he says, moving closer to me and launches into his speech. He isn't missing a beat.

Maybe I can change that.

Obviously, I don't want him to screw-up and embarrass himself in front of all these people, so I time my touches to the moments when he reaches a natural pause, or takes a second to look down at his notes. I take my own sweet time. The whole idea is to make him ache for it, the way he did to me back in the audience only a half-hour ago until he decided to bring me to a climax. I jerk him for quite a bit, before I so much as even flutter my tongue against his head. He is rock-hard before I wrap my lips around him.

Then, as soon as I do…I go to town.

I slip my mouth down over his cock.

Above me, he sucks in a sharp breath. It's not too obvious that it can't be passed off as anything more than taking a moment to think, but he looks down at me as he does so, and his eyes are wild and glittering.

I widen my eyes in a "who-me?" gesture, then flick my tongue against the underside of his cock as I slide my mouth up and down. He feels warm and smooth in my mouth, and I love the power I have over him in that second.

How things have changed, huh, Luke?

He continues with his talk. The slides keep changing. I know the presentation runs for about twenty more minutes, and I want to make him come right when it's over, so he can lose himself to the moment. In the meantime, I'm happy to torment him, to taste every inch of him until I know every ridge and vein of his cock.

I move my mouth up and press my lips to his head for a sloppy kiss, before running them down the underside. Then, I shift down inside his pants and catch his balls in my hand. Last night I didn't get a good look at them. I was drunk and it was dark. Today I see them clearly. They are large and cleanly shaven, and I swear to God, I lick my lips as soon as I lay eyes on them. I widen my mouth, and lower them to his testicles, taking each one in my mouth and lovingly lapping at it as I slowly jerk his cock with my hand. I run a hand down his leg, and find it solid with tension beneath his suit.

Good. This is exactly how I want him.

I move back up to his cock-head, and flick my tongue out against his tip over and over again. I taste pre-cum on my tongue, the salty-sweetness that tells me I'm doing a fine job, but that's not enough. I want it all. I want that power. He tightens his grip on the lectern above me, and I watch as his fingers tense on the wood at my every touch. God, I want this man. I want to make him come in my mouth, right here, right now. I still can't quite believe that this is me, thinking these things.

I hear him reaching the end of his speech, and I could have

sworn he is rushing, as though he has figured out my game. So I return my attentions to his shaft, tightening my lips around him, sliding up and down. I massage his balls lightly with my hand, letting my nails trail over his sensitive spots. If I'm not mistaken there should another paragraph of closing stuff, but he is already on his round-up. I lick, suck, touch, and play for all I'm worth. I'm determined—no, I'm desperate to make him come at the height of the applause.

And, to my great pleasure, he does.

I hadn't realized how tense I was until I feel him unload on my tongue. I wanted this just as badly as he did. As the applause starts up, he reaches down and wraps my hair around his hand, holding me in place as he thrust hard into my mouth. His cock pulses as he finishes, and I keep my mouth sealed around him, swallowing every drop that comes out of his wonderful cock. I look up at him, watching as he desperately tries to keep a straight face.

How do you like it, huh?

He nailed his speech, and I made him come. What could be better? I stuff his cock back into his briefs, zip him up and withdraw myself back behind the curtain.

"Thank you," Luke says and moves away.

The man who introduced him earlier is back to thank him and tell the audience that they have a fifteen minute tea break.

I hear the murmuring of the crowd as they leave their seats and start to disperse. I peep out from the parting in the curtain. The stage is empty. I crawl out, stand and walk away casually.

Luke is talking to a group of people. He is nodding, but his eyes are watching me. His cheeks are flushed.

I smile at him and wait quietly until he has finished with everyone else.

He walks up to me. His eyes are shining. "I can't believe you did that."

"Yeah, well, I can't believe you fingered me in a crowded auditorium," I shoot back.

"You deserved it."

"So did you. Did you like it?"

He grins. "It's always been a fantasy of mine," he says, as he leads me offstage.

"Oh, yeah?"

"Yeah," he confirms. "You just have a way of reading my mind, baby."

"That's what makes me such a brilliant assistant," I tease.

CHAPTER 12

LUKE

We arrive at the nearby beach resort quite quickly. Well, nearby if you take a helicopter, which is how we traveled.

"I can't believe you," Jade says, burying her toes in the warm white sand.

"What? Don't you like it here?"

She looks up into my eyes, the sea reflects in her eyes, making them appear green-blue. "I love it. It's just, you made it clear that we weren't on vacation. I didn't think I'd be able to explore the city, much less come all the way out here to this island beach."

I shrug. "I think we've had as much fun at the conference today as we could. I thought we could use a change of pace."

She licks her lips and it sends a jolt through me. "No arguments here."

"Good. Come on." I lead her up the beach to our private

cabana right near the water. During the ride over, I made a phone call to the friend who owns this private resort.

We walk up to the cabana right near the water. It has been beautifully prepared for our arrival. Everything we could possibly need for a day at the beach is laid out for us beneath the palm frond roof. A waiter from the resort stands there in crisp white linens, holding two frosty drinks in hollowed out melons.

"Ooo thank you," Jade says as she takes one. She takes a sip, and her eyes nearly roll into the back of her head. "Oh, my God, this is amazing. You have to try this, Luke."

I grab my own drink.

The waiter nods politely, and moves away. He stays close enough, so we can call him easily, but far enough away to give us our privacy.

I take a sip. "You're right. This is very good."

"How much alcohol do you think is in it?"

"I think you don't want to know."

She shudders. "I don't think I could bear another headache like this morning."

"Don't worry, we'll take it easy."

With her drink in hand, she sits in one of the padded loungers facing the water.

I sit on the chair next to her.

The sun bathes my skin, but the salty wind coming off the water keeps it from feeling sweaty-hot. The sound of the waves hitting the beach is soothing. Tension drains from me as the peaceful surroundings seep into me.

"When was the last time you did something like this?" Jade asks, turning to look at me.

"What? Sit on the beach with a beautiful woman?"

Jade shoots me a sour grin, like she thinks I'm being cheesy, but the flush of her cheeks tells me she appreciated the compliment. "No, I mean, when was the last time you just sat back and relaxed like this?"

The question catches me off guard. "You know, I honestly can't remember. I guess it's been a while." I take another sip of my drink and think about it. I really can't think of the last time. "You know how it is, with work and everything. The wheels of business don't stop turning long enough for me to take a vacation."

She sighs. "I know. Things are non-stop with you. But doesn't it feel nice?"

"It does," I admit.

"Then why don't you take a break every once in awhile?" she asks, turning to look at me.

It's such a simple question, but I don't have a good answer. "I've really never thought about it. I've always been driven, I guess. I know that if I work hard, I'll be successful."

"Well, yeah, but you're already successful by any standard. You've done it. You've got more money than God, offices all over the world, and an army of people working for you."

"True," I reply.

"So what's the endgame? When is it all enough? When can you sit back and enjoy your life?"

"Christ, Jade, you make it sound like I'm a miserable workaholic."

"No, not miserable. But you don't seem happy, either."

"Work makes me happy."

She nods. "Sure, but there are other kinds of happiness."

"Are there?" I ask, laughing.

"I mean, there could be. What makes you happy? Other than work."

"I've never really stopped to think about it." I drain the rest of my drink as I think. The answer is not at the bottom of my melon. Finally, I shrug. "I don't know."

"See? That's why it's good to slow down every once in awhile. It helps put things in perspective. Helps you figure out what you really want."

"And what do you want?" I ask, wanting to get the damn spotlight off me. These questions make me feel uneasy, like there's a part of me that's missing.

"I want lots of things," Jade replies. "The career, of course. But I also want a family someday. A couple of kiddos running around. A man I love."

"That's all so predictable," I retort.

She sits up straighter, bristling at my comment. "It may be predictable, but at least I have goals. Things to look forward to and to strive for in my life. What are you looking forward to? Adding more zeroes to your bank account?"

I don't have an answer. It's rare for me to be speechless like this, but here I am. Nobody has this effect on me, but Jade manages to throw me off-balance with ease, like it's nothing.

Jade stands up next to me. "I'm going for a swim." She strips off her flowing beach dress, revealing a jaw-dropping, itsy bitsy white bikini underneath. Her full, ripe breasts threaten to spill out of her top. I sincerely wish they would. Her bottoms are fitted enough that I can just make out the outline of her pussy before she turns around. I don't know if she sways her hips on purpose just to torture me, or if it just comes naturally to her, but I get rock hard just looking at her walk to the water's edge. My eyes stay glued to her firm, round ass as it bounces with every step.

Part of the reason I wanted to come to the beach was for this exact moment. Even though I'd already seen her naked, I'd been drunk. I remember everything that happened between us the night before, but now, in the brilliant light of day, Jade looks so much brighter and more vivid than my blurry memories.

The other reason I wanted to come out here was to spend some time alone with her without anyone else around. I'm still conflicted about sleeping with my assistant or whatever is going on between us. So I don't want all of my business colleagues there to witness it.

I'm not ashamed of Jade. I'm ashamed of myself for succumbing to the tired old cliché of the executive and his secretary on a 'business' trip in Thailand. It makes me feel like an asshole. No one would understand how amazing Jade is. They wouldn't think, "Oh, maybe he really likes her." They would judge her the way I judged all the women my associates brought along to these types of conferences.

I couldn't bear to have them think of my Jade like that, not unless I know it's worth it. But it's way too early to be sure about any of that yet. All I know about her is that I enjoy her company and she's so damn gorgeous it hurts to look at her. For now, that is enough.

Jade stands in the water. The waves come up to her knees. She turns around and waves to me, beckoning me like a siren. "Are you coming?" she calls.

I shrug off my worries with my clothes and run out to join her.

CHAPTER 13

LUKE

We get back to our hotel suite, and I'm still feeling relaxed in a way I haven't felt in a long time. It wasn't just taking the time to slow down at the beach. It's Jade. She has this effect on me. She makes me want to slow down and appreciate life. And in this moment, I'm a very appreciative man.

"I'm going to take a shower," she says over her shoulder as she walks toward her bedroom.

I slip off my damp clothing, and I hear the shower turn on in Jade's room. I glance down the hall to see her bedroom door standing wide open. Interesting. I pad down the hallway and look into her room. The bathroom door stands open as well.

If that's not an invitation, I don't know what is.

Jade is in the shower. I see her clearly through the transparent shower door. The water is steamy but it hasn't clouded up the glass yet. She stands beneath the shower head with the water cascading down her naked body.

I've been ogling her all day at the beach, but seeing her naked has my heart hammering in my chest like I'm about to have a heart attack.

Her wet skin glistens in the light, giving her an otherworldly quality. Like someone so perfect shouldn't even exist. But there she stands, mesmerizing me. Her eyes are closed. I'm glad she can't see me. There's no hiding the affection I feel for her. It must be written on every line of my face,

She arches her back, thrusting her breasts out. They're full and heavy, and I want nothing more than to take her hard nipples in my hungry mouth. The urge to join her builds inside me, but I don't move. I have to savor this moment. She's so goddamn sexy it makes my chest hurt.

Jade turns underneath the cascade of water, giving me a fabulous view of her round ass. It's like a firm ripe peach that I want to take a bite out of.

Slowly, she spins around and catches me watching her, lusting after her. Her eyes widen seductively, as her hands trace the lines of her naked body. My cock is at full attention. A sly smile spreads across her lips, and she beckons me to join her with one white finger.

I yank the door open so hard, it sounds like it might come off the hinges. I don't care if it does. The hotel could be on fire and it wouldn't stop me.

Our bodies collide. Her skin is hot and wet against mine. She slides against me, setting every cell in my body on fire. I lean down to kiss her. Her lips are soft and pliable. She parts them for me. Our tongues twist together, like our bodies are doing.

My arms wrap around her, and our legs mesh together. My cock presses against her hip, gliding along her skin with every movement. Just the light friction is enough to make my breath come heavy in my chest.

Her pussy pushes against my thigh. I flex my leg muscle instinctively, and she rubs herself over me. The heat coming from between her legs is hotter than the steamy water from the shower.

I run my hands over her slippery skin, tracing every soft curve like I'm trying to memorize it for later. She feels so good, better than the memories of the night before. Even though I've had a few drinks at the beach, I'm nowhere close to drunk. Although the touch of her body against mine is intoxicating.

I reach between us to cup her breasts. They feel like they're on fire. My hands circle her globes, my palms scraping over her pert nipples. Jade moans at the feeling and the sounds of her pleasure drives me crazy.

My hips move against her with a mind of their own. I'm so hard it feels like my cock will explode. Every beat of my racing heart sends a deep throb through my length.

Jade seems to notice because she reaches down to grip my cock in her warm hand. She strokes me from tip to base.

I grit my teeth and groan. Her touch is electric, sending jolts through my entire body. I bury my face in her neck and suck at her tender flesh. My teeth grazes over her skin. Her head leans back in ecstasy and she moans. The sound of it sends a shudder through me.

Her hand caresses my cock as I trail kisses down her chest

and take her hard nipple between my lips. I swirl my tongue over it, teasing her. My fingers pinch her other nipple. She strokes me faster, and my body feels like it's vibrating from the sensations she is awakening in me.

I reach down to grab her wrist.

She pulls away and looks at me. "What's wrong?"

I shake my head. "If you keep doing that, I'm not gonna last."

She smiles seductively, which doesn't help the uncontrollable ache in my cock. "So, what's wrong with that? I want to make you feel good."

"You're doing a hell of a job of that," I say, giving her a quick kiss. "But I'm not ready for that. Not yet."

"Oh, yeah?" she asks playfully. "So then you wouldn't want me to do this?"

Before I know what she's talking about, she drops to her knees and takes my cock into her mouth. Fuck, she feels so good. My jaw clenches and my whole body tightens up. I want to stop her, but her mouth feels like heaven around me. She's bobbing her head up and down over me, and instead of pushing her away, I tangle my fingers in her hair and guide her to the perfect tempo.

My hips pump against her face. I can't control it. Jade takes all of me, and there's no more holding back. My entire body tenses and shakes. I shoot hot streams of cum into her throat. But she doesn't stop. She licks and sucks at me, finishing me off completely.

I'm too sensitive now. It feels so good it hurts. I have to pull away. My hands grab her arms and lift her up, so she stands in front of me. I kiss her deeply, groaning at the aftershocks running through me.

I pull back and narrow my eyes at her.

She gazes back at me with a challenge in her eyes.

"I'm gonna make you pay for that," I warn her.

Jade nods. "You fucking better."

I turn the shower off and throw her over my shoulder. Her legs flail, and she squeals in surprise, but I hold her tight. I march her over to her bed and stop to give her a couple of playful spanks on her ass. She moans, and I feel her body quivering against me.

I throw her onto the bed. She lands on her back, her breasts jiggling in a very satisfying way.

Jade stares up at me, not afraid, but definitely uncertain about what's coming next.

But I know the answer to that. *She's* coming next.

CHAPTER 14

JADE

Luke grabs my ankles and yanks my ass to the edge of the mattress. I yelp at the violent motion. He's so strong and dominant. Totally overpowering me. I knew I was asking for trouble by making him come before he wanted to, and now he's going to pay me back.

He kneels between my legs.

Planting kisses along my sensitive skin, he starts just above my knee and works his way up gradually.

Every place his lips graze over lights me on fire. He licks and nips at my flesh, sending electric shocks directly between my legs. Liquid heat pools in my core, and I moan uncontrollably.

This is his revenge. He's taking his time, torturing me with pleasure.

Tension ratchets up inside me as he glides farther up my leg. His mouth teases my inner thigh now, and the ache between my legs makes me crazy. I need more. I burn for it. My whole body trembles with desire. My hips shift toward him, urging him to kiss me where I need it the most.

But Luke takes his time, clearly setting the pace.

"Please, Luke," I beg. "I need to feel you."

He ignores my pleas, but an evil smile curves his lips. He knows exactly what he's doing.

I can't stand it anymore. I need release. I reach down with my hand to take care of business myself.

Luke's hand snakes out and secures my wrist in a vice grip. He gazes into my eyes and shakes his head. "No cheating Jade."

I try my other hand, but he's faster. He has both of my hands clamped in one of his, keeping them away from my aching center.

I groan in desperation. "That's not fair," I cry out.

I try to press my thighs together, but Luke blocks the way with his body. I writhe over the bed, frantic for some kind of sensation between my legs. But there's no relief for me.

Luke is in total control. "I told you. You're mine, Jade. All mine."

"Yes. I'm yours. All yours. Just please, I need to feel you." I've never begged for anything like this in my life, but there's no stopping myself.

Luke edges up my thigh, getting closer and closer. My hips thrash forward, trying to get to him. But every time I do, he pulls back, forcing me to wait.

I'm almost sobbing in desperation now. All I can do is wait for him.

Finally, his head is poised just above me. His warm breath flows over me, but it only makes me ache more. His tongue brushes my clit and I fucking explode.

White-hot fire erupts inside me, filling my body with a pulsing glow. I buck wildly on the bed, filled with the most intense pleasure I've ever felt in my life.

Luke watches me come, his eyes dark with satisfaction. He releases my wrists. I'm still reeling from my orgasm when he plunges his head between my legs.

His tongue runs up my seam, ending at my hard clit. It swirls around my sensitive bud, and the pressure is back inside me. Even though he just made me come so hard I barely knew my own name, I need more of him. I'm not even close to satisfied.

Luke puts his whole mouth over me like he's sucking on a ripe peach.

It feels like heaven. I tangle my fingers through his hair and pull him closer to me, urging him on. Pleasure rockets through me. His every touch feels so intense after the slow burn he forced me to endure. Nothing has ever felt this good.

Until he slides his thick finger inside me. I almost shatter into a million pieces. His mouth still works my clit while his finger caresses my silky folds. It's a potent combination.

And the fact that it's Luke doing this makes it all the more exhilarating. Less than twenty-four hours ago, we were just boss and assistant. Now, I don't know what we are. Although, to be honest, Luke still feels like the boss with how completely he controls me and my body.

Pleasure spirals up inside me, making me dizzy, removing all rational thought from my brain. My whole world narrows down to the sensations Luke awakens between my legs. He pushes me closer and closer to the edge, and then I go hurtling off into space.

A wave of ecstasy washes over me. A low, animal moan escapes my throat, and my body quakes from the feeling. I can't think. I can't breathe. All I can do is ride the wave as it sweeps me away.

I collapse on the mattress. My heart beats too fast, and I can't catch my breath. "Holy shit," I manage to say. "Holy. Shit."

Luke now stands by the bed, watching me. I can't help but notice the hard length of him jutting from his body. Apparently, I'm not the only one who enjoyed that performance.

He grins at me. "It's not over yet." Luke presses his body over mine. The thick head of his cock nestles against my throbbing pussy. He slides against me, putting delicious pressure on my pussy, but avoiding my clit, which is still throbbing and incredibly sensitive.

I shift my hips up into him, hungry to feel him.

Luke leans down to kiss me, long and deep.

I moan into his mouth, savoring the connection between us.

Then he plunges his cock inside of me.

My head presses back against the bed, and I groan at the feeling of him filling up the empty ache between my legs.

He starts slow, working into me with long, smooth strokes.

I feel every hard ridge of his cock inside me. Even after coming twice, this feels amazing. It's different. He's hitting new parts of me and awakening new sensations. My breathing is ragged. Every thrust of his cock elicits a moan from my lips.

Luke smothers those moans with a kiss. His hands find mine on the bed, and his fingers intertwine with mine.

I gaze up at him, and his sapphire eyes lock on me. It's like we're joined physically in every possible way. There's a deeper intimacy to it. It's a feeling I can't explain, but I feel it in the marrow of my bones.

He pounds into me with a steady, maddening rhythm. Intense pleasure builds inside me with every stroke of his amazing cock. A raging torrent floods through my veins as my hips buck beneath him, meeting his every thrust, letting him bury himself deeper and deeper inside me. I feel my control slip away. I can't hold back.

Pleasure sizzles through me like a bolt of lightning. I scream his name as I come. My body clenches around him. His hips jerk one final time, and he spasms inside me, filling me with his hot cream.

Everything else in the world falls away in that moment. It's just the two of us, joined together in ecstasy.

Luke rolls off of me and sweeps me into his arms. I rest my sweaty head against his masculine chest. I hear the rapid pounding of his heartbeat. It matches my own. We lie like that for a long time, not saying anything. Just lost in this perfect moment.

I wake up at dawn. Luke lies next to me in bed. The sheet has shifted right down to his hips and in the blue light from the alarm clock, his naked skin looks like marble. He looks so peaceful lying there, his chest rising and falling in a steady rhythm. I lift my head and study his face. His features are serene, his eyelashes are thick and luxurious against his cheek.

God, how can any man be so splendid?

In that moment, something becomes crystal clear: I'm falling hard for Luke Remington. The reality of him is totally better than any of the fantasies and dreams I had about him. And the more time we spend together, the more infatuated I'm becoming. Every smoldering look he sends my way, and every lingering kiss just makes me fall deeper and deeper in love.

Who can blame me?

He is literally everything a woman could ever want in a man. Gorgeous, successful, powerful, rich, amazing in bed. But more than any of that, he's actually got a tender, sweet side to him that he doesn't usually show. He's perfect.

Okay, he does have some faults. He's possessive, jealous, and domineering, but funny thing is, I actually like those things about him. I like that he takes total control of our relationship. That he wants me so badly, he can't stand to see another man flirt with me. It's like the pull of a drug thinking that he wants *me*.

When he could have almost any woman in the world. Every single woman he's dated has been a knockout beauty. I mean, perfect tens. They are the kind of women featured in magazines. The kind of women who are so physically perfect, you hate them just for existing. He never dated them for long though. Most of them, he went out with once, and that was it.

I'm a far cry from those perfect women. I look in the mirror and I see imperfections galore. If even perfect wasn't good enough to keep him interested long term, how full of myself would I have to be to think I could be the woman to change him?

No, I'm not insane. I recognize that things between us won't last once we get back home. Luke will want to make things professional again, probably citing his rule about not dating the women he works with. I'm not even sure I'll still have a job when I get home, much less, him.

The only way to keep from getting my heart torn to ribbons when this inevitably blows up in my face is to keep reminding myself in the days to come that no matter how much I want it, all of this is temporary. What we have is just a fun indulgence for him while he's out of the country and away from his real life. This trip isn't supposed to be a vacation, it just feels like a vacation kind of romance. Something that burns hot and bright, but then fades almost as quickly as it began.

So what if Luke and I are temporary?

I'll make the most of the little time we do have together. If nothing else, this trip will be a cherished memory in my old age. A memory of that wild and wonderful week in Thailand when I was young, carefree and in love with the most amazing man on earth.

That alone should make this relationship worth it.

I curl up against Luke. My body melds against his, and I savor the warm feeling of his skin. Just being close to him banishes my troubled thoughts. *This* is real. This right now, being in bed with Luke, cuddling up against him, and feeling the soreness between my legs from what we did last night. This is happening. While his skin is against mine like this, I can pretend that it's not going to completely devastate me when this is over.

All my fears about tomorrow are just fears. I'll deal with them tomorrow. I am here right now next to Luke.

No matter what the future holds, I won't let it ruin the present.

I close my eyes and listen to his heart beating as I fall back asleep.

When I wake again, Luke is walking out of my bathroom with a towel wrapped around his waist. Water glistens on his skin, and my chest aches at the sight of how handsome he looks.

"I could get used to waking up like this," I comment.

Luke leans over the bed and kisses me. His skin is warm from the shower, and I breathe in the clean scent of him like a drug. I moan into his mouth.

He pulls away from me with a sigh. "No more of that, or we'll never leave the room today."

I stretch on the bed, letting the sheet slip down to reveal my breasts. "And what's wrong with that?"

He grins and shakes his head. "You did that on purpose."

I shoot him a sultry smile. "So what if I did? Are you going to come back over here and punish me?"

He groans at my words. It sounds like a low rumble in his chest, like the sound of distant thunder before a storm. "You have no idea what you're doing to me."

"Why don't you show me?" I ask.

His hands grip the edge of the towel, and it drops to the floor. He's naked, and his cock hardens under my gaze.

I lick my lips. I'm fascinated to see the physical effect I have on him.

I roll over to the edge of the bed nearest to him. My hand reaches out to slide along his shaft, coaxing it fully to life. Then I grip his length and gently pull him toward me. The moment he's close enough, I dip my head down and plunge him into my mouth.

I might not know what the future holds, but I know that at least for today, he's all mine.

And now he knows it, too.

CHAPTER 15

LUKE

I leave the suite with a spring in my step, feeling like the king of the fucking world. How can I not, after Jade's surprise blow job? It was a hell of a way to start the day. Although, just waking up next to her was pretty great, too.

I don't like sleeping with women. It sends the wrong message. Creates an illusion of closeness for them and fuels expectation. It bit of being cruel to be kind. I *fuck* them and send them on their way as soon as possible. Most of the time, I don't even bring them back to my place. Hotel rooms are easier. If they don't know where I live, then there's no risk of them showing back up in my life unexpectedly. There's no putting a price on peace of mind.

But I just can't seem pull myself away from Jade's body. Our rooms are separated by only a lounge so it's not even like it would be any trouble to part ways. The first night, we were drunk off our asses, so that night doesn't count, but last night...I was fucking stone-cold sober.

And we were in Jade's bed as well. I could have slipped away to my own room at any point without it being weird. So, why didn't I?

Jade continues to surprise me, and not just with morning blow jobs. I've broken two of my rules for her. I never fuck the women I work with, and I never sleep with women I fuck. But this is the second night of mind-blowing sex I've had with my assistant.

It doesn't bother me that I've broken the rules for her, and the fact that it doesn't bother me is a surprise, too. Jade is different somehow. She's worth it. My mind wanders back to last night and the amazing sex we had. I can't *stop* thinking about it. God, she is something else. She really knows what she's doing. She comes off innocent, like she doesn't have a clue, but the fact is she's got a fantastic body, and she knows how to move it in just the right way to drive me out of my mind.

I freeze in the act of knotting my tie and stare at my own reflection.

Jesus, am I getting serious about this girl?

I frown. I mean, I feel like a brand new me, and when she isn't around, I can't stop thinking about her. And I cannot bear the idea of any other man even looking at her. Is this it? Is this love? Hell, I don't even know how she really feels about me. Maybe I should take her out on a real date and explore how she feels about me.

I slip my wallet into my trouser pocket, and cross the lounge to knock on her suite door. Suddenly, the anticipation of what I'm about to ask her sweeps over my body. It's an odd feeling. Clammy hands, shortness of breath. I feel nervous, which is another first for me. I never feel nervous when asking women out. It's second nature to me. Like buttoning a shirt. What is wrong with me? Maybe, I'm coming down with something.

Jade opens the door in her bathrobe. "I can still taste you," she says, and licks her perfect, plump lips.

"Do you know what happens to little girls who tweak the tiger's tail?"

She shakes her head, her eyes big and solemn. "What?"

"They get taken out," I reply.

Her gorgeous hazel eyes sparkle like the ocean waters, and I feel as if I am drowning. "Like on a date?"

She's teasing me, and it's cute, but I don't think she realizes how serious I am about this. "Yeah, like on a date."

"Like a *date*, date?" She repeats, her eyes widening.

"Yes, although I'm not really sure what other kinds of dates there are. You could—"

She grabs my face. "Stop talking," she mutters and kisses me deeply.

It causes my cock to twitch, even though I just got a blow job. "So that's a yes?"

"Well, I'll think about it," she says with a shrug, and takes a step away from me.

I grab her arm and pull her toward me, making her body slam into mine. We stare into each other's eyes. It's driving me crazy that she just won't say yes. But it's making me want her more. "I'm serious," I state firmly. "Will you?"

"Okay," she answers nonchalantly. "What time?"

"Seven."

"If you aren't here at seven, I'll be at the hotel bar drinking myself to death because you stood me up."

"Oh, yes," I say with a laugh. "I'll be here. 6:55."

"You do realize you just jinxed yourself, right? Now you will be late." She laughs.

I realize how much I really love the sound of her laugh. It's almost contagious. Just like her gorgeous smile. "I'll be here. I promise."

I spend the rest of the day thinking about our date. It consumes me. My stomach is churning, and I'm beginning to think that I might have picked up some bug when it finally hits me that it's nerves. I'm not accustomed to this feeling, which is why it took me so long to identify it.

I've never been this nervous before in my life. Not even for my first date. I guess it's because I've never really given a shit about a girl before. I want everything to go well with Jade, and I'm worried I might fuck it up somehow.

I'm outside her door by 6:40. Which makes me fifteen minutes early for our date, but I'm too eager to wait any longer. I knock and she answers.

"Now you're too early," she scolds, smiling that dazzling

smile at me. Most of the hair on the left side of her head isn't curled. Shit, I *am* too early. But she still looks gorgeous. "Sorry, I'll get a drink and wait out here."

"No, no. Get your drink, but come in and talk to me while I'm getting ready." She waves me inside.

I pour myself a whiskey. The anxiety buzzing in me is at an all-time high, and I can't seem to calm my jackrabbiting heart either. My jangled nerves are unusual, but I guess this whole situation is unusual for me. Jade has done the one thing no other woman ever has. She makes me give a damn.

When I go back into her room, she has already curled the other half of her hair. I sit on the couch and watch her in the mirror as she puts on her makeup.

"Did you get the email I sent you about Roberton and Payne?"

"Uh…huh." I've never watched a woman paint her face. Quite fascinating the trouble they go to. Still, the effect is stunning.

She paints her lips last. Fire-engine red. She smiles slowly at me. "Now I've just got to slip into my stockings."

My eyebrows rise.

She stands and lifts her foot up to the padded stool she was sitting on and rests the tips of her toes on it. Then she gathers her stocking into a bunch and begins to slip it over her toes. Loads of women have given me strip shows, but no one told me watching a woman get *into* her stockings could be so damn sexy.

Hell, it's almost an art.

By the time she pulls the nude gossamer fabric past her calf and it reaches her thigh, all of it being done through the gap in the front of her bathrobe, I am rock hard. I take a big gulp of my drink and try not to look so hypnotized.

From underneath her bathrobe she finds the clip of the suspender belt and expertly attaches it to the stockings. When she lifts the other leg to repeat the procedure her action parts the robe and I see her pussy covered in white satin. I walk over to her and rip the bathrobe off her body.

My eyes greedily devour her breasts in her white lacy half-cup bra, before I push her back down on the padded seat.

"We'll be late," she protests.

I don't even bother to answer as I fall to my knees. While looking into her eyes, I take the stocking from her hand. Grabbing her foot, I copy her action and slowly pull the thin material up her smooth leg. The clasp is a bit fiddly for my big fingers, so she pushes aside my hand and fixes the straps herself. I grab both her ankles and open her legs wide. The crotch of her panties are soaked.

"Hold your legs open," I order.

"Luke," she cries, but she obeys my instruction and keeps her legs wide apart for me.

I push aside the silky material and look at her pussy. I watch her dripping for me. And it is fucking beautiful. I slide two fingers into her wet core.

"Oh, God," she groans. "Don't, Luke."

I place her stockinged feet on my shoulders and burying my head between her legs, licking herjuicy fruit.

She stops protesting and claws her fingers into my hair instead.

I don't lift my head again until she has climaxed into my mouth and I have licked her clean.

"There," I state with satisfaction. "Now you're ready to put on your dress.

Her chest heaves. "I'm never getting dressed in front of you again. You're an animal."

She has no idea. What I really want to do is throw her on the bed, turn her meticulously curled hair into a tangled mess and have her lipstick all over my cock. "Hurry up, or you'll really see what an animal I am." I slap her open pussy and she snaps her legs shut. I stand and walk back to the couch. I have such a hard-on I can't watch her get dressed anymore. I go outside to the lounge and refill my glass. I hear a sound and turn around.

She is standing at the doorway of her bedroom dressed in a slinky black dress and very high heels. She is at least three inches taller than normal. Her shoulders are bare except for thin straps. The dress is not tight, but every curve of her body is on display. I think of all the men who will look at her and feel a tightening in my gut. I squash it down. They can look, but I'll be the one taking her home and fucking her senseless.

"Wow," I exclaim softly.

"Now, you're just exaggerating," she retorts, making a face. This time, she sounds as nervous as I feel.

"You know me better than that. I never exaggerate," My heart is thumping in my chest.

She smiles. "Yeah. You're not one for exaggerating."

"That's right." I stand and walk over to her. "Are you mine, Jade Emerson?"

She looks up at me. Her eyes shiny and enormous. Her plump lips part. "Yes."

"No flirting with other men?" I murmur.

She shakes her head. "No."

"Only me?"

"Only you," she confirms softly.

"Good. Because I don't want to punch anyone tonight."

A slow smile spreads across her face and her voice is teasing and playful. "So, you're saying we're like, *together*?"

An unfamiliar feeling of affection radiates from my chest making me feel wonderful. A smile forms unbidden on my face. "Is that what you want?" I ask.

She shrugs, but humor dances in her eyes. "Hey, you're the one talking about me not flirting with other men. Your words, not mine."

I test the waters. "I can take it back if that's what you want."

"You better not," she says seriously. "I belong to you, remember?"

I nod. Satisfaction fills me at her response. I'm not used to feeling this way. It's new but good. So much for not being impulsive.

I lightly brush my lips with hers and her perfume fills my

nostrils. God, she is intoxicating. If I stand here a moment longer, we're going nowhere. "Let's go."

Downstairs, we leave the great glass door and the balmy tropical night envelopes us like a long-lost friend. There is excitement in the hot air. My blood drums in my ears as I watch Jade climb into the waiting limo.

CHAPTER 16

LUKE

It is lovely and cool inside the limo. I uncork a mini bottle of champagne and pour it into a pair of fluted glasses. She watches me from beneath her lashes. Her thigh is touching mine. I hand her a glass.

"We're like what, ten minutes in?" she asks. "And you're already trying to get me drunk?" She shrugs. "It works, I guess." Her laughter bubbles up like the champagne in her glass, and it's just as intoxicating.

"I don't need to get you drunk. Behold last night and this morning," I counter, grinning at her.

"Touché." Tipping her head back, she slams the whole thing.

I take a sip and watch her. I'm trying to understand why she gets under my skin the way she does. Why her?

She opens a lidded container. It has little canapes. She bites into it delicately. "Mmm...lemon grass and chicken."

"Let me taste," I urge.

"Get your own. I'm not sharing."

"I don't like to share, either," I say, my voice low.

She knows exactly what I mean, and I watch a smile cross her face. I can tell she might just like me as much as I like her.

We get to the restaurant, and I help her out of the limo. Inside, a hostess in traditional costume puts her palms together and leads us to a table. There are palm fronds all around us. Every head turns to look at us. We must look good together.

The wine list is not the best I've seen, but I order a light Muscadet to go with our high spiced food.

"To us," I say, lifting my wine glass.

"To us," she echoes.

The delicate way she sips her wine is driving me crazy. Everything she does is sexy to me. She could snort when she laughs, and I would still find it charming as hell. "You're fucking sexy, you know."

"Oh please," she says with a laugh, but then she licks the rim of her wine glass.

It's something that many a woman have done to tantalize me, but when she does it, it pierces right to the heart of me, sending desire surging through my veins. I want her bad. And I want her right now.

I picture ripping her dress off and sucking on her gorgeous tits right in the middle of the restaurant. Laying her on the table and eating her out for dinner and dessert. My cock stirs in my pants.

"What?" she asks, a single, delicate eyebrow raised.

"Nothing."

"No, tell me," she prompts.

"What if I don't want to?" I tease.

"Well then, I guess we won't be having sex anymore," she says,

I stare at her. Surrounded by ferns and greenery she is like a seductive nymph. "Why is that?"

"If you can't tell me what you're thinking, then I can't let you into my pants." She shoots me a seductive smile.

This girl is killing me, and I'm loving every second of it. I'm starting to think that this thing between us might just work out after all. The food arrives and it is delicious. I do that thing I never do. I spear a morsel of food on the end of my fork and hold it out for her.

She takes it between her lips. Her eyes watching me. Oh, sexy.

Then she flutters her eyelashes comically and laughs at herself.

I laugh too.

We have so much fun together, and for the first time, I want more of that in my life. Fun. But not just any kind of fun. Fun with *her*. Fun where we go back and forth, teasing each other. Fun that makes everything we do together exciting and new, even if it's not the first time we've done it. Her stockinged foot slides up my leg.

God, I want this woman.

I excuse myself from the table and go to the restroom. I've got to adjust myself because the conversations we were having, the thoughts I've been thinking, and her wandering leg, have given me a painful erection. This is definitely not the sort of place for me to be showing it off.

As I re-enter the dining area, I run into a business associate from way back, Matt. We weren't close or anything, but we've hung out outside of work before. I haven't seen him for years, and I almost didn't recognize him.

"Luke-fucking-Remington," he says loudly, clapping his meaty hand on arm.

"Hey, man," I reply, surprised to meet him in Bangkok of all places.

"How the hell are you?"

Alcohol fumes hit me in the face and I lean back slightly. "I'm good. Really good, in fact. What are you doing here?"

He grins broadly. "Business, of course. Like there's anything else? What about you? Is this business or pleasure?"

I shrug. "Business, mostly."

He gives me a skeptical look. "I didn't recognize you from the back before, but if you're with that hot chick over there, I guessing she's the eager little assistant, and you're dipping your pen in the company ink, huh? You dirty dog, you." He laughs at his own joke and slides his eyes over to where Jade is sitting. "I don't blame you. I wouldn't mind a bit of that ass myself."

I'm not laughing. My stomach is churning. I hate the way he's talking about Jade. As if she's nothing. A piece of meat. And like I'm hanging around her just to get laid.

My whole life, I've had issues with relationships because my dad cheated on my mom with his bimbo secretary. It broke up the family, my mom never got over it and I hated my dad for it. It's been weighing heavily on my mind ever since I saw Jade in that towel, but I've pushed the thought away more than once when she and I are together.

But to have someone else echo my own doubts, even as a joke, is like getting hit in the balls with a speeding baseball. I've spent my whole career making sure I didn't get involved with anyone I worked with and what do I end up doing? Exactly what my father did. I'm banging my secretary. Worse, I'm imagining all kinds of feelings to camouflage the fact that I'm just like my dad. Weak and without real principles. All my great protestations were only good while there wasn't real temptation. As soon as there was one, I fell for it hook, line and sinker.

I scowl at Matt.

Even though he's hammered, he senses the shift in my mood. "Hey, I was only kidding, dude. I didn't mean anything by it."

"Whatever, man," I say, pushing past him. I make my way back to the table. I'm done with him, and I'm done with this dinner. And I'm done with Jade. It's not just about my own reputation, although that is a serious issue for me. It's about hers too. Everyone will look at her the way Matt just did. They'll think of her as slutty and cheap, when she is anything but those things. I like her too much to let people treat her that way. I can't do this with her. I've been fooling myself. We're away. In a hot country. We're both attractive and we just lost our head. But the fun clearly has to end, for her sake and mine.

I walk up to the table. "We need to go." I hate the cold sound of my voice, but it's the only way I can get through this.

A flicker of surprise crosses her face. She doesn't ask why. She simply sets her glass of wine down and stands up, so we can leave.

I don't blame her for the confused expression on her face. I didn't really explain to her what caused my sudden mood shift. I don't want to explain it. And I don't need to.

I'm coming off like an asshole, but my run in with Matt has me shaken up. He made it impossible for me to carry on pretending that what I'm doing is okay. Why the fuck did I have to run into him tonight? It ruined my good evening, and now, possibly even ruined things with Jade forever. I'll never be able to look at this situation the same way again.

"Is something wrong?" she asks, as we walk out of the restaurant.

"No," I say, trying not to snap at her. It isn't her fault that I'm upset. I'm the bad guy here. I'm the fool who let things get this far. I have rules in place to avoid situations like this, but I stupidly broke those rules for Jade. My father must be laughing in his grave. Wait until you are in my shoes, then let's see if you can walk away, he told me once when I begged him to come back to Mom. I spat in his face and told him I'd never be like him. Never.

Well, Dad…

She is my assistant. And I made a mistake. She's beautiful and I got carried away. But I'm not going to carry on letting my dick decide

my life. I'm not you. Not now. Not ever. I won't let that happen.
I'm better than you.

I know I'm hurting her, but in the long run, this will be for the best for her too. She deserves better. I'll just end up breaking her heart and almost certainly hurting her career if I keep going with this. I could never live with myself if I did that.

I'm aware she wants to know what's going on. Jade has a baffled expression on her face. I just can't be with her. It's not right for either of us. I just hope I can make her see that without tearing her heart to pieces like mine is right now.

CHAPTER 17

JADE

The limo pulls up to the curb five minutes after Luke calls the driver. Five minutes that seems like five hours of uncomfortable silence. I feel embarrassed by the way he rushed us out of there. Like I'm a child who threw a hissy fit in a grocery store and had to be yanked out by an adult.

The driver opens the door up for us. I get in first while Luke stands waiting for me. I'm surprised he does something so gentlemanly, considering his clearly agitated state. He gets in after me, and we pull away from the curb.

We sit in the limo, drowning in silence. There's no laughing or playful banter. It's completely different than the ride to the restaurant. It's as if a different person is now in the limo with me. Someone cold and distant. Someone I really don't know at all. Something is seriously wrong. He was fine until he went to the toilet. Did he get a phone call when he was in the bathroom? Was it business related? I want him to tell me what's going on. He's hiding something.

"What's wrong?" I ask him. It's the third time I've asked, but I can't help it. I won't just settle for 'nothing'. It's tearing me apart that he won't just tell me what's happening.

"Nothing," he repeats. There's a bitter tinge to his voice.

This is driving me crazy. Tonight, I felt myself get ready to take a ride on cloud nine. Now, I don't know if things between us are heating up or cooling down. If this doesn't work out, I'll have to quit my job and move away. I'll have to start all over.

"Please, Luke. Just talk to me. Tell me what's wrong." I'm not trying to sound like I'm begging or anything, but desperation creeps into my voice. He's totally shutting me out, and I don't know what to say to get through to him.

"It's really nothing, okay?" he says, staring out of the window.

I'm getting more and more upset with him. Is it too much to want to know what the hell is going on? One moment everything is hunky dory and the next, he has become this cold stranger. My mind goes into overdrive. Maybe he went to the restroom because he was having second thoughts about me. Or he suddenly realized he didn't actually like me, after all. Maybe this is what all the women in his life get when he is done with them. Maybe it was all in my head. I was always just another notch on his bedpost.

This last thought hurts, and the pain motivates me to keep pressing him.

"Can you please tell me what the hell is going on?"

Luke ignores me. He just stares out the window, avoiding my gaze. Like this is just some fling he's had, and he desperately wants me to go away. This is bullshit, and I want to call him out on it. I want to tell him he's being a complete asshole, and I don't deserve this shit. Not from him. Not from anybody. Maybe I just shouldn't care. Maybe I should turn cold and distant like he is. But I *do* care, dammit.

Plus, the way he spoke to me really bothers me. I turn my head to look out the window, puzzled and hurt. I just want to get back to the hotel and not have to deal with any of this.

I feel his hand on my leg, and whirl my head around to look at him.

"I'm sorry," he says softly. "It's a long story, and one I have never shared with anybody. It has to do with my father."

This issue, whatever it is, is clearly personal and painful. I want to place my hand on his to comfort him, but I don't because my feelings are still hurt. I don't want him to feel like I'm pressuring him, but I *do* want to know. I want to know what his father has to do with me. "Will you tell me?"

Luke winces, then looks out the window, like he can't face me. "When I was little, I looked up to my father. He ran his own business like I do now. It was nowhere near as big as mine, but it was a respectable size, and he was respected in our community. Then, he had an affair with his secretary and when my mom confronted him, he simply ran off with her." He shakes his head bitterly at the memory. "What my father did was awful. It tore my mom apart. It tore our *family* apart. When people found out, they treated my mother like a joke. Like it was somehow her fault. And they treated him like a joke. He was that cliché fucking businessman chasing skirts at the office and banging his secretary. Ever since then, I've had my rule about not dating people who work with me. I refuse to follow in his footsteps."

I take a deep breath, as I try to process it all. I'm glad he opened up, but I'm not really sure what else to say to him. Even if he is having some kind of internal crisis, the way he's treating me still isn't fair. So, he has some issues from his past with his father? I don't understand what this has to do with me, or why he feels the need to treat me this way. None of this is making any sense to me.

"Because I never wanted to repeat the sins of my father."

I'm not really sure how he expects me to take this. It feels like a knife to the back. I don't really know what to do. It's easily the most hurtful thing I have ever heard in my life. And possibly, the most heartbreaking.

"Fuck, this sucks so bad. I don't know what to do with these feelings I'm having."

Pride comes to the rescue. "Pleeeeease, don't uproot your principles for my sake," I say sarcastically, and scoot myself away from him. I stare out the window, picturing how the night could have gone had he not freaked out like this. We could be sharing dessert right now, or getting ready to leave. We could be headed for a stroll, or just headed back to the hotel to screw each other's brains out.

Instead, we're sitting here in this icy silence. So now, for the first time since we got here, I feel homesick. I feel ready to go home. But we still have two more days here. Two more God-awful days. Neither of us speak for the rest of the ride back to the hotel. When we get there, we walk inside and ride the elevator together in silence. I stare at the lighted floor numbers. What is there left to say? Obviously, he's made up his mind and I'm not going to beg.

I can feel him staring at me. His gaze is boring into me. I try to ignore it and focus on the elevator passing each floor.

Only four more to go until ours.

I have never felt so uncomfortable in my life. I hate every second of the ride.

Three more floors.

I just want out of here. I don't want to be standing next to him any longer.

Two more floors.

Hurry up, I silently urge. We're almost there, then I can be away from him.

Just one more floor.

Evading his look, I pull my cardkey out of my purse. As soon as we reach our floor, I step out of the elevator and go to our suite. I shove the key into the slot as fast as I can and open the door. I get inside, dash across to my bedroom, and close it quickly.

I lean against the door feeling so hurt, so angry. He led me up the garden path, with his bullshit about being his. He made a fool of me. Tonight, he actually made me think we could be together. That he might actually be falling for me. If he has such a big problem being with me, he should have never let things get this far. He should never have allowed this to start in the first place. I hear his footsteps move to his bedroom and his door shut.

"Fuck this," I mutter.

How could he? He led me to believe tonight was an actual date. That he really wanted to be with me, but here we are, further apart than ever. For the first time since we've arrived in Thailand, we are sleeping in separate bedrooms. Unsteadily, because I am so devastated, I walk to the bathroom. In the mirror, my eyes looked crazed. Blankly, I remove my makeup and get out of my designer knock-off. I was so in love with it. I had such high hopes when I picked it out to wear tonight. Now I hate it. I'll never be able to look at it again and not remember tonight's humiliation and hurt.

I take off my stockings and suspenders then nearly sob with the memory of how he ate me out this evening. God, how stupid I've been. I climb into the big bed. The bed I shared with him the night before. I turn my head and I swear I can smell him. His cologne, his skin. It's too much. I don't think I can sleep here tonight. I grab a pillow, pull the blanket off, and make my way over to the couch. I'll sleep here. Far away from any reminders of him.

I punch the pillow a few times and lie my head on it. For an expensive hotel suite, the couch is awful to sleep on. I guess nobody ever thought someone would try to sleep on it. I know it has a pull-out bed, but I'm not going to put the work into getting it pulled out and situated. I'm too mentally exhausted. I know that I won't be able to sleep tonight.

I think back to the first day he hired me. I remember thinking to myself that I was going to have a hard time keeping my hands off him. For two months, I did just that. Then, I come on this trip with him and almost every single one of my fantasies came true. I was so close to what I thought might be a fairytale romance. Maybe that's the problem. They are fairytales for a reason. Girls eat them up because they want it so bad, but in reality, there are no prince charmings. Just bosses that use you and throw you to the curb without explanation.

I grab my phone. It's ten in Bangkok, so it's nine in the morning in New York. I could call my best friend Emma. I need someone to talk to. She might be sleeping, but maybe she'll wake up.

I dial her number. It rings and then goes to voicemail. I don't want to worry her, so I leave a generic sounding message. "Hey, Emma. Just checking in. From Bangkok. I still can't believe I'm here. Anyways. I'll try again later. Miss you."

I hang up the phone. I have no one to talk to. I'm hurt all over again, and I feel even more lonely. I punch the pillow again and try to go to sleep, but it's impossible. The tears are threatening to take over and drown me.

"No," I snarl. "I'm not going to cry."

Because more than anything, I don't want to cry. Crying is a sign of weakness. I'm just tired and need sleep. Maybe if I can sleep on it, I'll wake up and won't have feelings for Luke anymore. Maybe I won't even remember his name.

A girl can dream, can't she?

My phone starts vibrating on my lap. I almost forgot I left it there. I pick it up and see that Emma is calling me back.

"Hey!" I say, trying to sound cheery. I don't want her worrying about me.

"How's jolly old Bangkok?" she asks.

"It's amazing," I say. A few hours ago, it wouldn't have been a lie. It is now.

I'm holding back tears. The sound of her voice is making me miss her and home so much more now. I just want to get back there and retreat to a time when none of this happened. Back in my old bed and my old fantasies about my boss. No longer having to deal with these feelings. In fact, I want to go back and choose to not apply for this job.

"What's wrong?" Emma asks.

"Nothing at all. Why?"

I hear her sigh. "Dude, come on. We've been friends for long enough. You think I don't know when something is bothering you?"

I take a deep breath and slowly let it out. Tears sting my eyes. I try hard not to cry. I don't want her to hear my voice crack. I clear my throat. "I'm homesick I guess." My voice cracks. Ugh. Now she's going to know.

"You're crying," she says. "What happened?"

"It's Luke," I reply.

"I'll kill him."

"Thanks, I appreciate the thought."

"Honey, before you carry on, I have to tell you the sex is never as good when you're sober."

I laugh through my tears. "No. It's not the sex. That was even better when I was sober." My voice cracks again. I really hate that.

"Then why are you so upset? Come on. Tell Aunty Emma what happened?" she prompts soothingly.

"I have feelings for him," I confess sheepishly.

"You think I don't know that?" She laughs. "I've known since the moment you told me you got the job there in Danny's Bar. Your eyes lit up like a Christmas tree when you talked about him."

"Really?" I wish I was better at hiding things. I wish I was like him.

"Yes, really."

"He asked me out on a date, tonight," I say.

"And it didn't go well?"

A tear rolls down my cheek. I dash it away. "No, it didn't."

"What happened?"

I tell her about the date and how well it was going, how he acted when he came back from the bathroom, and what he said about mixing business and pleasure because of his dad.

"Now I feel like a complete idiot," I finish.

"Sweetie, this is all on him. If he's got some weird daddy issues, he should have stayed away from you. He especially shouldn't have asked you on a real date. Listen, I've got to get to work. I'm running really late. But don't let that son of a bitch get you down. If he's too scared to be with you, that's his loss not yours."

"Thank you, Emma," I say.

"No problem."

We hang up, and I instantly feel alone again. I felt better when I was talking to her, but now that the loneliness has sunk in once again, my heart is starting to hurt all over.

I know it's going to be a long night for me.

CHAPTER 18

LUKE

It's morning and bright outside the window. I didn't get much sleep last night. The way the night ended with Jade drove me crazy. I wanted to say more to her, but everything I could think of saying felt like it would make me sound even more pathetic than I already am.

I don't feel good.

I kept mulling over how things could have been different if I hadn't run into Matt last night. Jade and I would have left and came back here. I wouldn't have been able to keep my hands off of her. Hell, maybe we would have even had sex in the limo. If we didn't have sex in the limo, we would have tumbled into bed together and went wild. It would have been amazing.

Damn Matt for ruining our night. The way he spoke about her made me see red. I overreacted and took it out on her. There was another way, a much better way to do this. I spring out of bed, shower, and leave the suite before Jade wakes up. I don't want to see her yet. I'm not ready to face her. I need to think and figure out what the hell I'm feeling.

I don't feel good.

I almost wish I hadn't brought her with me on this trip. That I could go back to the uncomplicated days when she was my plain PA. So fucking drab sometimes, I didn't even know she was there. The job just magically got done. Fuck! I really am a bastard.

I go downstairs to the restaurant and all I can think of is being here with Jade. I look at the long buffet table heaped with every kind of breakfast item imaginable and find that I can't even face the thought of food. I pour myself a cup of coffee, find a seat at a table facing the large windows, and go back to thinking about Jade.

Maybe it was a good thing I ran into Matt. It woke me the fuck up. I don't want to be like my father, but I am starting to be more like him. How on earth did I get to this point? It's pissing me off.

Then I think about how she looked last night, right before we quit talking. Her face fell. She looked as if her heart broke. I never intended to do that. Not to beautiful, sexy, smart, funny, amazing Jade. I put my coffee cup down slowly and stare incredulously out of the window.

Oh! Jesus! I'm in love with her.

There is no doubt about it.

I'm in love with Jade Emerson.

What happens when I take her back and people find out I'm dating my assistant?

The knives will be out for her. They are going to say that she gets special privileges because we are together. I can weather the storm, but it'll destroy her reputation. I think about my mom and how her friends all acted like she had some disease. It wasn't her fault that my dad couldn't keep his dick in his pants. I don't want Jade to go through what my mom had to go through. No one deserves that kind of torment. No one.

People are going to talk. It's what they fucking do. They're lives are so goddamn boring, they search for any kind of drama to gossip about. They don't know how to mind their own damn business. I don't want our relationship to hurt Jade in any way. I need to sit down and talk with her.

I stand up to go back upstairs and run into Mr. Hatanaka, one of the Japanese businessmen.

"Remington San. Just the man I was looking for." He holds his hand out to me.

I firmly grip his hand and shake it.

"Mr. Hatanaka, it's good to see you. I hope you're not here to deliver bad news."

I laugh. He laughs, too, but I think more out of courtesy than because he actually found my joke funny.

I'm a little nervous that he is here in my hotel looking for me. I did not expect him, or anyone from his company, to reach out to me so soon. I don't know whether to take it as a good or a bad sign. I've been so consumed with thoughts of Jade and what I should be doing with her, for the first time in my life, I've actually put my business on the back burner.

"I would like to discuss with you the opportunity you presented us with the other night," he says, nodding gravely.

Discuss the opportunity? I thought it was a done deal. I keep my expression neutral and interested. "I was just leaving, but if you would care to sit down, I'll be happy to go through any details that you are still unclear about."

"Please. That would be excellent," he replies.

With a smile, I indicate the chair across from me. He sits, clasps his hands on the table surface, and looks expectantly at me.

It's hard to read him when he isn't smashed. The other night he was slapping my back and regaling me with dirty jokes that he would tell, then immediately apologize to Jade for telling them. This morning, his mouth is set in a straight line and his lips are pressed firmly together. His facial expression screams that he is in work mode.

"Can I get you something to drink? Coffee?" I offer.

"No. Thank you."

"Right. What is it that you wanted to discuss?"

"We are happy with the figures you drew up for us. They are perfect, and your company sounds like the kind of company that we would like to develop a partnership with."

This sounds like good news, but I don't want to count my chickens just yet. If they are so happy with my figures what the hell is he doing here? I don't want to be disappointed.

Like I've disappointed Jade.

The thought comes out of nowhere and causes me pain. I push down the strong urge to simply leave this blathering idiot here and go up to apologize to Jade. I've been so caught up with my own drama, I've hurt her. I force myself to concentrate on what Mr. Hatanaka has to say.

"So...we want to sign with your financial company," he continues with a big smile. "We think that by going with your company, you can lead us in a newer, more innovative direction. A direction that we can see our company thriving in. Yours as well, of course."

"That's great news." I plaster a big, happy smile on my face. I'm still waiting for the catch. For the 'but' with some added stipulations.

"Yes," he says. "I'm excited to be working with you and your company. I know you'll bring great things to us."

"Oh, I will. You don't have a thing to worry about." I know I sound cocky. But I hope he takes it as confidence. "I'll have my lawyers send over the paperwork to you."

"I look forward to hearing from them," he says with a polite nod.

A waitress approaches our table and asks if we need anything. Mr. Hatanaka dismisses her politely, telling her that he's just getting ready to leave. I wave my hand to indicate I'm fine, and she walks away.

Mr. Hatanaka stands up. "I'll be sending a gift over to your room soon, to honor our newly formed business relationship," he says.

I stand to shake his hand one more time. "You don't need to do that, Sir," I say. I flash my 'I'm-a-good-guy' grin. I'm weird about receiving gifts.

"In Japanese culture, we do not deny our friends the pleasure of giving," he says this with a smile.

I nod my head. "It's a good practice. Thank you. It's very kind of you. I'll be looking forward to your generous gift."

We say our goodbyes, and I watch him leave. Then my brain immediately switches back to Jade. I want to tell her about the impromptu meeting I just had with Mr. Hatanaka. She was crucial in landing this deal, so I know she'll be over the moon. But the way things are right now, she'll probably slap me in the face before I can even open my mouth.

I get up and head back upstairs. A group of smiling, chatting conference attendees wait by the elevators. The last thing I want is to be stuck in a confined space with them while they try to strike up a conversation with me.

I hang back then get into the next free elevator. The doors close, and I'm thankful to be alone inside the elevator car. The elevator comes to a stop on my floor. I get out and go straight to her door. I rap on it. There is no sound from inside. I turn the handle and step into her room. She's not in it.

This is driving me insane. I want to talk to her. I want to kiss her. I want to tell her I know I acted like an ass last night. I want to tell her that I've never felt this way before and it scared the shit out of me. I want to tell her how sorry I am for hurting her. Then I want to tell her I love her and want to be with her. No matter what, we'll work it out.

I pull out my phone and call her, but her's is switched off.

I pace the floor. Well, she has to come back. All her things are still here. I decide to get started on my talk for the following day. I sit down on my bed with my laptop, but I can't concentrate. My inspiration is gone. Jade isn't here to help inspire me. And it hurts.

At that moment there's a knock on my door.

"Finally," I mutter. Thank God, Jade has more sense than me. She's making the first move to crack the icy wall between us. I rush through the lounge and pull the door open.

"You're not Jade," I say, a frown creasing my brow.

CHAPTER 19

JADE

Luke and I haven't spoken since last night, but he is speaking at the conference tomorrow, and I still have a job to do. So I woke up at four am and I've spent all this time arranging and preparing for that. It didn't help keep my mind off of Luke, though. I've thought about him non-stop.

I wonder what he's doing. Is he thinking about me? Does he feel bad? Probably not. Why would he, after the way he treated me? You don't treat people that way if you care about them. It's obvious he doesn't give a damn about me.

I want to talk with him and work something out.

I walk into the elevator and ride up to our floor. I step out, and as I'm walking down the hall the door to our suite opens and a local girl with long black hair and a pink mini skirt steps out. Her heels are at least six inches high. She's tarted up like she's going to a club, but it's the middle of the fucking morning. My insides burn with jealous rage at just the sight of her.

What the fuck is going on?

She closes the door softly and starts walking towards me in her high heels. She's got that cat got the cream look on her face. The look I see in the mirror after Luke has fucked me good. She would have passed me by without even a glance if I had not stopped in front of her.

"Who the hell are you?" I'm aware that my voice is hard and cold and I'm being mean, but I can't help it. I hate her.

Her dark eyes flash. "Who are you?" she asks me cockily.

"Did you just have sex with him?" I ask her.

She gives me a sly smile. "Which guy?"

"The guy in that suite? Did you fuck him?" I don't want to play games. I just want to get to the bottom of everything. If she says yes, then I'm fucking done with Luke Remington. The moment I get back to New York, I'll walk away and never see him again.

"It's none of your business."

I'm so angry I feel like punching her smug face. I've never wanted to punch anyone before. She's smaller than me. I can take her. I grab her hand. "If you don't tell me, I'll report you to the hotel. How would you like that?"

A flash of fear passes her eyes before she masks it. "Yes, I did," she admits defiantly. "Happy now?"

It's the exact opposite of how I feel.

"Let go of me. It's not me you have to be angry with. It's just my job," she says quietly. And suddenly, I feel ashamed of myself. She's such a small thing. Even in her ridiculously high shoes, she only comes up to my chin. It's a wonder to think that Luke's big cock could possibly fit inside her. The

140

thought sickens and disgusts me and I immediately release her.

She straightens her top and walks away without a care in the world.

I'm still staring at the empty space where she was standing when I hear the elevator doors close behind her. Only then, I realize I haven't moved since she said she had sex with him. I don't know what I expected, but it wasn't to hear her actually say yes, but she did.

She has no reason to lie to me.

But I don't get it. Luke and I have a fight and he buries his cock in a fucking prostitute?

My heart feels like it is shattering in that hallway. The pain runs deep and sharp. This kind of misery in my heart is new to me. I've never experienced it before and I don't want to feel this way. I don't want to think any more about Luke fucking her. I don't want to think about him anymore at all.

I honestly feel like I could punch a wall. Or maybe his face. I want to go into our suite and confront him. I want to look into his eyes and ask him what makes him think it's okay to fuck a hooker after last night. What makes him think it's okay to sleep with anyone after the way we've been with each other? But just the thought of the ensuing arguments makes me feel exhausted. I'm so done right now. I'm so angry and hurt. I wonder if I can find a new job before I get back to the states. Would it even matter?

What I need is a drink.

Yes, if I just get a drink in me, or several, I'll be able to make it through the rest of this miserable trip until we head back to the states. I'm so over Luke, this trip, and this whole fucking country right now.

I turn around and head for the elevator. My mind is so scrambled I don't register the ride down or the walk to the bar. Suddenly, I find myself sitting down at the bar and ordering a vodka with a finger of tonic. The bartender fixes it up and sets it in front of me. I drink it and order a second one. He doesn't so much as raise an eyebrow. I drink that down and hit him up for another. I don't want to think anymore. I want to feel completely and totally numb.

"Hey, Jade," a deep, masculine voice says from behind me.

I turn to see Carl Magnus in all his Viking glory. His long blond hair drags over the shoulders of his suit jacket, and he looks like a fusion of ancient and modern man.

I'm surprised. I really didn't think I was going to see him again. Especially after the way Luke had acted toward him the other day. "Hey, Carl," I say glumly. "What brings you here?"

He sits down on the bar stool next to me. "I'm day drinking today," he replies with a laugh. "I don't think I can make it through another boring speech unless I get a little buzzed. What's your excuse?"

"You know, I'm not usually a day drinker." I finish my third drink.

The bartender points, and I nod my head. He gets to pouring me a fourth one.

I haven't eaten much today, and I know I need to pace myself. I need to make sure that I don't go over my limit and totally embarrass myself. I'm still on a business trip, whether or not I'm with Luke. I still need to be professional.

Carl nods. "What happened, if you don't mind me asking?"

The bartender serves me my drink, and Carl orders himself a straight Jack Daniels.

Should I tell him? Does he really need to know what's going on between Luke and me? I bet he would love to hear that we aren't working out. That Luke is off fucking everything that walks while my heart breaks more and more. I imagine myself taking Carl up to my room just as Luke is leaving his. He'll get mad, and I'll say, "If you can fuck whoever you want, so can I." I almost burst into a mad giggle. I'm starting to feel quite light-headed. Maybe a bit crazy too.

"Well, I've realized something that I think might actually be pretty awful," I say.

"What's that?" Carl asks.

I take a sip of my drink. This one tastes more like tonic than it does vodka. I make a face. The bartender must think I'm a lightweight and can't handle my alcohol. I finish the drink, fully aware I left Carl just hanging. I turn back to him. "I'm in love with Luke."

"I'm well aware. It was the reason I hit on you. I like you. And I could see that a good dose of jealousy would do Luke good."

"What? You knew I was in love with Luke that day?"

"Of course. I saw it a mile off."

"How?"

"The way you were looking at him, but I know Luke is a

tough nut to crack. He was fighting it, so I decided to help you by giving him a little push." He grins. "I figured he'll owe me, then."

"No, you don't get it. We aren't together. I'm in love with him. He couldn't give a shit about me."

Hearing the words aloud is a kind of a revelation that I cannot ignore anymore. They couldn't be truer if I pulled them out of a law book. We aren't together. We never have been. And I shouldn't be letting him get to me, and drinking my woes away at a hotel bar. I should be out sight-seeing and enjoying myself. I've finished everything I had to do for today. But even the thought of going sightseeing on my own makes me feel depressed.

"You still aren't together?" Carl asks, surprised.

CHAPTER 20

JADE

I shake my head glumly while he slips the bartender money. I'm pretty sure he just bought me a drink, and I wonder what Luke would think if he saw it. Actually, I know exactly what he would think. He would think that Carl is trying to take me away from him. In the past, he would have got mad, but now I guess, he won't give a shit.

"No, we aren't together," I say with a heavy sigh.

He frowns. 'Why not?"

"It's a long and pathetic story."

"It can't be worse than the lecture I should be listening to."

I suppose it can't hurt to talk to him. For some weird reason, he seems to be on my side. "First of all, thank you for trying to help me." I wrinkle my nose. "By pretending to hit on me."

He nods to acknowledge my gratitude.

"As you guessed, I've been secretly lusting after Luke for months now. Anyway, it all kicked off during this trip and we kinda started sleeping together. We went to a beach, and he asked me out on a real date last night, and I thought we were getting on really well. So he takes me to this really nice restaurant, and then in the middle of it, he wants to leave. So, we leave and when I force him to tell me why he was being such a dick, he told me this awful story about—"

I realize I'm rambling and stop before I tell Carl too much. As mad as I am with Luke, what he told me about his father is an intensely personal secret. Luke may have betrayed me by fucking someone else, but I won't betray him. I skip over that part.

"Anyway," I continue, staring down at my drink. "He basically told me it's hard for him to be with me. I told him if he doesn't know what he wants, then I can't do this. So we haven't spoken since then. I left to do some last-minute things for a speech he is giving tomorrow. I come back to the suite and there's a hooker leaving his room." I say the word "hooker" way too loud, and it makes me cringe with shame. I look around to make sure no one heard me.

Carl chuckles.

"What?" I ask. "I don't really see what's so funny. My heart is broken. I'm sitting at a bar, day drinking with a guy who almost got his shit rocked for pretending to hit on me. There's no humor in any of this."

"You really love this man, don't you?" he asks quietly.

I nod my head.

He looks at me and really studies my face. His eyes are so green and piercing they make me feel nervous and uncomfortable. Like an insect struggling on a pin.

"Well, you need to give him a chance," he states casually. Like it is the most natural thing in the world for me to simply gloss about last night's fiasco and forget about the hooker.

I stare at him in shock. "You do realize I said he just *fucked* a whore, right?"

He laughs again.

"I'm glad you find it hilarious, because my heart feels like it's been shredded to ribbons," I snap.

"You need to let that go," Carl says with a shrug of his massive shoulders. "You said you weren't together. So technically he didn't cheat on you. Sometimes when a man is scared of something that he knows is good for him he turns to what's familiar instead."

I shake my head with disgust. "Just trust a man to stick up for another."

"Come on. I'm on your side. The thing about turning to what is familiar is that it never works. What have you got to lose? You love the guy. Give him a real chance and let him prove his love for you. If he fails, you can be miserable then."

"Love for me? Have you heard a word I've said? He doesn't love me. He doesn't even want to be with me. He won't tell me anything. To get the story about his dad was like squeezing blood out of stone." I wave my hand around my face. "He's put this wall up between us. I can't get through, no matter what."

"Trust me, that man loves you," Carl says stubbornly. "I could tell when he called me out when he thought I was hitting on you. I saw it in his eyes."

I think about how Luke acted when Carl hit on me. Carl could be right. Luke's reaction that day was more than just jealousy. It could have been love, too. It makes me smile, and I'm starting to feel a little better about everything. Also, the alcohol is making my head buzz. "I don't know how to get him to open up to me. I know you say that he loves me because of how he acted. But maybe that's not love. Maybe that's just lust and possession. A kind of crazy."

"Isn't love just a happier version of insanity?" he asks and takes a drink. The ice cubes in his drink clink together as he tips his glass back. He sets it on the counter and looks at me. "If you want to know the truth, you have to confront him. You owe it to yourself to be brave."

"I wish it was that easy,"

"Best form of defense is attack. So go in, all guns blazing."

"You know, you're kind of easy to talk to. Like one of my girlfriends."

He laughs. "It's the long hair, isn't it?"

I smile. I really like him. "Maybe. But there's not one single feminine cell in you. No one would mistake you for a woman. You're all man."

He grins. "Well, there goes my dream of being a drag queen."

We both laugh at that.

Carl motions to the bartender. "Another round for the lovely lady and me, please."

The bartender mixes us up some more drinks. I know I shouldn't drink anymore. The first ones are starting to hit me hard. That last sentence came out all slurred, but I figure

I'll stop after this one. I'm sure I can handle one more without anything bad happening. I've finished all my work, all I have to do is crawl upstairs, and go to bed. Alone.

As I sit there morosely sipping my drink, Carl regales me about his life. How he climbed Mount Everest. His story is fascinating, and he's a good storyteller, but I can't stop thinking about Luke. I'm disappointed that he never even tried to call me. When I look at my phone I see that it is turned off. I turn it back on, but there are no texts or voice messages.

Suddenly, the alcohol hits me hard, and it's all too much.

"Are you okay?" Carl asks me.

I shake my head. I'm trying hard not to cry. That's the last thing I want to do in front of him. In front of anyone, really.

Carl offers me a gentle look, at odds with his hulking stature. "What you need to do is finish your drink, go upstairs, and knock on his door. Tell him you want to talk to him, and that you aren't going to leave until he, as you Americans would say, damn well talks to you." He pauses and raises his eyebrows. "But he has to really talk. It can't just be him mumbling that he doesn't know how he feels. It's time for him to man up. Don't let him get away with that bullshit again."

It's good advice. And he's being friendly. Like legitimately friendly. Not how guys are when they want to get in your pants, or because they think you have great tits. He's being a good human being, and I love that.

"Thank you for talking to me," I say. "I know I've said that already, but seriously. You've helped me feel better. I've really needed this. I'm in a foreign country, and it feels like I'm all alone."

"You are welcome. And don't worry, little Jade, Luke will come around. You'll see. He can run, but he can never hide from his love for you."

I smile gratefully at him. I do feel a little better. But I know I won't feel totally better until I am able to get Luke to sit down and actually talk to me. And if I can't, then that's on him. That will be his own problem.

I finish my drink and set the empty glass down on the table. "Do you think I should go upstairs now?" I ask my new-found confidant.

CHAPTER 21

LUKE

I pace my bedroom floor restlessly. I was glad the hooker came by when Jade wasn't around. It wouldn't have been a pretty sight. But where the fuck is Jade now? I've already been to the conference hall, the room upstairs where all the other PA gather to do their clerical work, the swimming pool, the three coffee bars.

Hell, I need a drink.

It'll help clear my head. I decide to go down to the bar, first. I head out to the elevator, and make my way to the closest drinking hole. I stop mid-step at the entrance of the bar. Carl Magnus at the bar, sitting next to Jade, and too fucking close, damnit. I don't like this. As I watch in stunned disbelief, the asshole slides an arm around her. My blood starts to boil.

"What the fuck?"

Now I know why she didn't answer. She's right here with the guy who was hitting on her the other day.

Mesmerized by the scene unfolding before my eyes I see

her laugh at something he says. I don't know what the hell is so funny, but I do know I'm going to put a stop to this once and for all. I've already told this guy to stay away from her.

She smiles at him and says something. He smiles back.

From where I'm standing, they are clearly flirting. I see red. It's all I see. My fists clench at my sides. She's my girl. I thought I told this jerk that already. And now here he is. As soon as there's a little hint of trouble, he comes sniffing around. Who the fuck does he think he is?

I feel sick and angry. All of my muscles are tense, and I'm grinding my teeth into dust. But I can't calm myself down. I'm seething with jealousy. I take one step, and then another, until I'm standing right by them. My fists are still clenched at my sides.

He is telling her some story.

Both of them are oblivious to me. He mentions Paris, and I know I'm about to punch him. I don't have time to listen to him telling my girl romantic stories.

"Carl," I say. I glare at him so he knows that I'm not here to play nice. He's trying to take what's mine, and I'm not going to let that happen. He's stupid if he thinks I'm going to let him take her from me.

He turns and looks at me. "Hey, Luke. Funny thing you're here."

"Oh yeah, why's that?" I ask, feeling even angrier.

"We were just talking about you," he says.

I look at Jade. She avoids my eyes, and that doesn't sit right with me. It makes me paranoid. Pain tears through me. Did I do this? Did I push her into the arms of another man?

I turn back to Carl. "You were talking about me? You think you can just sit here with my girl and move in on her because we had an argument?"

"Luke," Jade says warningly.

I don't respond to her. I'm too focused on Carl right now. I want to knock his stupid teeth out.

"You've got it all wrong," he says and stands up.

My clenched fist collides with his jaw before he can say anything else. He stumbles back and trips over his bar stool. Carl Magnus doesn't fall to the floor like a demolished skyscraper, he rights himself, shakes his head and grins at me. That stops me in my tracks and the fact that Jade screamed. I grab her hand and pull her through the lobby. People are running over to make sure that Carl is okay, and I just wish I had knocked him out cold.

"Let go of me!" Jade shouts.

Totally ignoring her, I drag her struggling body into the elevator with me. Someone tries to come in with us and I glare at him. He steps back immediately. The doors close. Finally, we're alone. I'm vibrating with fury. I can feel my muscles shaking from how tense they are.

Jade looks really angry, too. When the elevator dings, she steps out quickly, trying to leave me behind.

I catch up with her in a single step, grab her hand, and take her into the suite.

I still don't know exactly what I want from her. And that

might be the worst part about this whole thing. I wasn't raised to talk about my feelings. I was raised to push feelings aside.

I close the door behind me and look at her. I'm not sure what to say or do, but she looks fucking gorgeous standing here in my bedroom. My dick twitches. I want to fuck her, but I know I'll get a knee in the nuts with the way she is feeling. Beside, we have things we need to discuss. Like her great idea of letting that douchebag buy her a drink and put his arm around her.

I feel myself getting angry all over again, just from thinking about her sitting there with him. The image of him touching her enters my mind, and it drives me crazy. I want to punch his face all over again. So much for being turned on. I cross my arms.

"What the fuck was that about, Luke?" she yells before I can interrogate her.

Her face is dark with anger. I've never seen her this way. She looks like she wants to punch someone, and I wouldn't be surprised if that someone is me. I deserve it after everything that's happened.

"You were drinking with him. He had his fucking octopus arm around you."

She gasps with astonishment. "I was having a civilized drink with him. He's the only friend I have in this country. He was comforting me."

"Comforting? Pull the other one. I wasn't born yesterday. You think I don't know what was on his mind. He was plying you with alcohol…" I stop, my eyes narrowing. Her chest is heaving and her cheeks are flushed. She's drunk! "How many have you had?"

"None of your fucking business."

"Everything about you is my fucking business."

"Let me get this right," she states sarcastically. "You get to be possessive over me, but I don't get to object if you fuck other women."

I scowl at her. "What the hell are you talking about now?"

"I'm talking about you having sex here in our suite with a fucking hooker!" She's so murderously angry she shaking.

CHAPTER 22

LUKE

I can see her fighting back the urge to break down. I stare at her in astonishment. How would she even know about that? Was she in her room all day? Spying on me? Not that I have a problem with that. It tells me that she really *was* thinking about me. I guess the woman had been dressed fairly whorish. It wouldn't take a detective to figure out what she was. Usually, this sort of misunderstanding would be funny, but right now, it's not because Jade looks like she's about to burst a gut.

"How do you know about her?" I ask.

"I ran into her when she was sneaking out, or whatever the hell she was doing. That's why I was down there drinking in the first place. Carl came out of nowhere, and he was being nice. He wasn't hitting on me."

"You've got it all wrong," I explain.

"I've got what wrong, Luke?" Suddenly, she sounds exhausted.

"I didn't sleep with her. You remember Mr. Hatanaka from the other night?"

"Ugh," she groans. "Was he in here, too?"

"No, thank God," I say, shaking my head. "I ran into him this morning at breakfast. He sat down with me. Your pitch worked. You sold him. His company is signing up with us. And he told me he had a present for me, and he specifically reminded me that rejecting a gift was rude."

"Yeah," she says. "But what does this have to do with your whore?"

"That whore was his gift to me. But I didn't do anything with her."

She scoffs. "Funny thing about your story."

"What's that?"

"She told me you *did* fuck her."

I laugh. "I paid her two hundred dollars to pretend that we did. I wanted her to tell anyone who asked that I had a great time. I didn't want Hatanaka to be insulted that I turned down his gift, as fucked up as it was. I had no idea you were going to have a chat with her. Otherwise, I would have told her to tell the truth if a beautiful woman named Jade asked what happened."

Jade narrows her eyes at me, but says nothing.

I sigh and shake my head. "Jade, I know I have a reputation for getting with a lot of women in the past, but none of them have been prostitutes. You know me. I don't do that. I've never done that. I don't need to pay for it." I look into her eyes. I need her to believe me because honest to God, I didn't sleep with Hatanaka's gift.

She hesitates and I see the doubt in her eyes. She doesn't believe me and that doesn't sit well with me.

"Jade, I know I've been an asshole to you. I know that I'm far from perfect. But I've never lied to you, even when the truth hurts. And I'm not lying to you now. I didn't sleep with her, Jade. I haven't even thought of anyone other than you since our first night together."

I need her to understand how much I love her, and how badly I've been wanting to fix things between us today. I don't want her thinking for even a second that I don't want to be with her, or that I want other women. Especially, not some bought and paid for prostitute.

"If that's true, then are we together or not?" she asks out of nowhere.

I wasn't expecting this from her.

I still haven't had enough time to figure out my feelings or what I want from her. I don't know if I can respond to her. At least not the way she wants me to right now. I'm still lost and confused about how I actually feel.

"Is this a real relationship?" she asks. "I need to know right now how you feel about me. I can't keep doing this shit."

She's on the verge of tears, and I have no idea what to do. I've never been through anything like this. Put me in any business situation and I'll come up trumps, but nothing in my life has equipped me to handle a situation like this. So again, I tell her the truth, even though I know it's not what she wants to hear. "I don't know," I say.

Her face falls, and the tears she was trying to hold back begin to slip down her face.

God, I must be broken inside if I can't just say what she wants me to say.

"You called me your girl downstairs, but now you won't even tell me how you really feel about me?" she asks. "You know what, Luke?"

"What?" I brace myself.

"If you don't know what we are, or if you can't be with me, then you can't act like this. Either I'm yours, or I'm not." She runs out of my bedroom and into hers. She slams the door shut behind her. The sound of her lock clicking closed is loud.

I feel so awful. I keep breaking her heart a piece at a time, and I'm not sure how to fix it.

I feel like a volcano about to erupt. I need to burn this excess energy off. Either I break down Jade's door and fuck her or I leave the hotel.

I walk down the street in the midday heat. My shirt sticks to me but the walk is good for me. It helps burn off some of this restless energy, and allows me to clear my head. Things with Jade are worse than ever. No wonder, I've stayed away from real relationships. This whole situation is frustrating and confusing. I can never seem to do the right thing.

I have embarrassed her twice now. I can't stand myself sometimes.

I see a liquor store. As I walk past it. I stop and go back to the entrance. Inside it's busy. I have to wait in line. I choose some unrecognizable brand of vodka because I don't really care. I might have a hangover tomorrow, but what the fuck? I deserve to suffer as penance for hurting Jade.

I don't open the bottle as I walk, because that's something my dad would have done. He was an alcoholic. A major one. He drank whenever, and wherever. I'm surprised he ever managed to run a business.

I swore I'd never be like him. I'm no a drunk. I've never even been a big drinker. And there are so many other differences between the man he was and the man I am. *I'm not him*, I repeat to myself.

I focus on that one thought because it's true, and I'm finally realizing this.

I don't have to fear everything that he did. I can fall in love with my assistant without thinking I'm as despicable as him. Unlike him, I'm not married to anyone. I won't be destroying anyone's life if I decide to be with her. Jade means everything to me. She's the woman for me. I don't care if I have to give up everything I have worked for all my life to achieve.

Jade is my life.

Screw what other people think and screw who my father was. I refuse to let that bastard fuck up my life any more than he already has. I never should have let my memories of him control me this way. I should have told Jade exactly how I felt yesterday morning.

I can still tell her before it's too late, but it's not enough to knock on her door and say the words. Words are cheap, and after the way I've behaved, they won't be enough. I have to show her in a big way how I feel about her, and in a way that leaves no doubt in her mind that I truly love her.

An idea comes to me.

When I get back to the hotel, I go up to our suite. I open the bottle and take a couple of swigs. It's cheap stuff and it burns my throat. I chuck it in the bin, and sit down at the table with my laptop.

CHAPTER 23

JADE

It's the last day of the seminar, and it's almost time for Luke's speech. This is the huge finale to the whole convention. Everybody will be there. Well, lah-di-fucking-dah, and good for him. He'll be the star of the show. I feel extraordinarily bitter today, as I should be. I don't know how I will sit there and watch him give his speech. I know this is my own damn fault for hooking up with my boss.

I won't be able to do this when we get back to the states. I can't be his assistant if he can't even respect me enough to tell me his feelings. He can't just keep stringing me along until he's ready to make up his mind about me.

I know he has feelings for me. Maybe not love, but certainly some sort of affection and desire for me. But the fact that he won't tell me bothers me. It's like he's ashamed he has feelings for me, and I think that part hurts the worst.

I stayed up half the night, crying and looking for a new job.

I walk into my bathroom, hoping I don't have to see him for the rest of the day. I don't want to talk to him. I just want to get through the rest of this trip and go home. I'm so over this entire episode.

Before we came on this trip, I wanted to be with him so bad that I would have sacrificed almost anything to make it happen. I would have done whatever he asked me to so we could be together. That had been a mistake. I never should have given my heart away.

I just want the pain, the hurt, and the anger to stop.

I want it all to go away.

There's a knock on the bedroom door, and I hold my breath, but it's obviously not important because there isn't another knock. There aren't sounds of him clearing his throat or any desperate declaration of love. My breath comes out in a rush. At this point, I have to admit that there never will be.

I turn the shower on, setting it all the way to hot. I step inside and quickly suck air in through my teeth. The water is almost scalding. It stings my skin like cleansing fire. It's a good way to burn away my feelings.

The bathroom is steamy already, and I haven't even been in for very long. I wash my hair and then my body, trying to free myself of what I'm feeling inside. Of what I'm thinking. I stand and let the water fall over my body for a long time. I'm soaking up the heat. I know I'll have to face him again when I get out.

Finally, when I can no longer put it off, I reach down, and turn the water off. I slide the glass door open and snag my towel off the nearby rack. The cool air sweeps across my naked, wet body, leaving goosebumps in its wake. I towel off and look for what I will wear.

It takes me almost an hour to get ready, but that's because I'm dragging this out. I have to go to his presentation, regardless of how I'm feeling. I have to sit and listen to the man I love talk to hundreds of strangers when he refuses to talk to me.

When I emerge into the lounge, I see that everything I laid out for his speech yesterday is gone, and so is he.

I wait until the last minute to head to the auditorium. I'm nervous. My stomach is in knots. *God, why am I so nervous?* I'm not the one who has to give the damn speech. I'm not the one that has to stand up in front of hundreds of people and make my company look good.

I walk over to the giant convention center that's attached to the hotel. My heart feels fragile as I think about how excited I was when we first got here. Everything seemed like such an adventure. My first trip abroad. Being with Luke. My heart had been so carefree and so full of expectation. I thought I was going to have fun.

I place my hand on my stomach. I still don't understand why I'm so nervous. I smile politely at people who smile at me as I enter the convention center. I'll die before I let any of these people know I'm not okay.

My eyes dart around the room. I don't see Luke, but I assume he's in the back somewhere waiting. He should be starting in just a few minutes. I find a seat towards the front. I wanted to sit in the back, but I know I need to be close, just in case he has issues with any part of his speech. Broken or not, it's still my job to be his assistant, and I owe him that much. I won't just leave him high and dry up there if things go tits up.

I only wait five minutes before someone comes up to the podium. It's one of the people we met when we got here. Something that now seems so far away. A distant memory that maybe one day I won't even remember, along with the rest of this trip.

The guy introduces Luke and the room claps. He's a big name, and everyone here has been looking forward to his presentation. I have to catch my breath when I see him. He looks so gorgeous, so hot, so distant. It seems incredible to think that I had sex with him. I woke up next to him. My heart starts to race. I hate that I have to stare up at him for the next hour or so when I cannot have him. My eyes fill with sudden tears. It's dark in the hall and I surreptitiously wipe my eyes.

He smiles at crowd before stepping up to the podium. "Good morning, ladies and gentlemen. For the three or four of you who don't know me, I'm Luke Remington, CEO of Omega."

A wave of laughter sweeps through the room. He's already got them eating from the palm of his hand.

"I'm so glad to be in this beautiful country, talking to you today. It's been an honor to come here, to learn about the culture, and meet a lot of cool people. Although I mostly came for the Thai food."

The crowd laughs again.

I look around at the hundreds of people here, all watching Luke. I wonder what it's like to stand up there and have all of them staring at you. It's got to be nerve-wracking. But Luke is as confident and commanding as he is in a personal meeting. Despite everything, I'm impressed.

"I know that I'm supposed to be up here talking about business," he says. "I'm supposed to make you guys trust me and like me. I'm supposed to make you trust my business. But there's something else I want to talk about. Something far more important."

I'm confused. None of this was in the notes I prepared for him. He's going off book, and it's really irritating me because I worked so hard on it. It's almost like he's kicking me when I'm down. Like, 'Hey, Jade. Let me stomp on your heart some more. This speech you worked so hard on is useless.'

I want to walk out of here and never look back. Instead, I stare at my nails, trying not to let my anger show.

"You see," Luke continues. "I came here on a business trip, hoping to get some new clients and expand my business. What I didn't come here for was love."

I freeze and look up at the stage. He's looking right at me. He found me in the dark! I'm not sure what he's doing, but I know I'm supposed to be listening. I continue to make eye contact with him while he continues his speech.

"Today, is a momentous day for me," he says. "Because I'm going to make an announcement to you all. I am madly in love with my assistant, Jade. And before everyone freaks out as to why this matters, I'll tell you why it matters. I hurt her. And I'm sorry."

I vaguely hear gasps and muttering from the crowd, but it's all white noise in the background. Tears sting my eyes, and I'm trying hard to hold them back. I don't want to cry in front of all these people.

"I hurt you, Jade. And for that I'm sorry, but I need you to know something." He looks around the room. "I need all of you to know something."

He gets off the stage and walks over to me. Whoever is running the stage lights follows him with the spotlight.

"I'm in love with you," he says, standing in front of me with the mic still around his head. "I love you, and I want to be with you. I'm ready to take the leap if you are."

CHAPTER 24

JADE

I feel hundreds of eyes staring at me, but I don't care, because the only eyes that matter in this moment are his. He gazes down at me, and there's no more fear or uncertainty there. All I see is love. And then his perfect lips press into mine.

At first, there is stunned silence, then the crowd goes wild. Cheering, clapping and whistling.

My heart feels as if it will burst with happiness as I kiss him back and cling to him desperately. In my kiss is everything I want him to know. I forgive him. I want to be with him. We pull apart because we're still in a room full of people.

He stands up tall and waves to the crowd. "Thank you all for allowing me to share this with you." Then he grins sheepishly and adds, "Um, creating wealth is great, but always follow your heart, I guess is my message."

He tosses the microphone to a guy standing nearby, and grabbing my hand, whisks me up the walkway toward the doors.

People are still cheering for us, and it feels amazing. It's the affirmation I needed.

We fly out the doors, back into the hotel, and into the elevator. The doors barely close behind us before we are all over each other. His mouth is on my mouth. His hands are on my body. He's touching me, feeling me, loving me.

I want him. I want him so fucking bad it hurts. I press into him, and I can feel his hard cock sinking into my hip.

He pulls back and looks at me. "I want to be with you. Fuck what my dad did and fuck whatever anyone else thinks. I was so stupid for doubting that things could work between us. I should have listened to my heart and never pushed you away. I love you, Jade. I love you, like I've never loved anyone or anything before."

"I love you, too," I say. Tears are falling from my eyes again. "Judging from the crowd's reaction, I don't think anyone thinks any less of us for being in love."

Luke gently brushes my tears away with the tips of his fingers and smiles. "I know. Trust me. I feel like a jackass that I ever thought they would. Can you forgive me?"

"After that speech, I suppose I can give you another chance to make it up to me."

The elevator doors open. He grabs my hand, and we run down the hall. He shoves the key card into the slot and throws the door open.

We go inside of the suite, and our lips lock together again. I hear the door close on its own, shutting us away from anything but each other. His hands rove over my body, touching me the way I'm dying to be touched.

He moves his hands to my ass and squeezes.

"I love this dress," he says against my lips. "But I want it off."

He spins me around so my back is to him, and his fingers clasp the zipper. He yanks, and the dress opens in the back.

The air feels cold against my flushed skin, and goosebumps pebble my flesh.

"I want you so much, Jade," he says as he helps remove the dress from my body.

I pull my arms through the sleeves and then shimmy out of it as he drags it to the floor. I'm only wearing panties since the dress has a built-in bra.

He gazes down at me hungrily.

"I want you, too," I whisper.

His palms graze my breasts, and I shiver. His eyes lock with mine, shining with love. "Not just like that," he says. "I want *you*. All of you. I want you to be mine forever."

I look down at where his hands are resting and laugh. "I want you, too. Forever."

He moves his hands to my waist and pulls me into him. "You're so perfect," he says, kissing me again.

I love the way he tastes. It's sweet, as if he had a piece of fruit with his breakfast this morning. Or maybe it's just that I've missed kissing him.

His hands slide down to my ass. He gives me a spank, and I jerk my body into him. He kisses me and pushes me at the same time, so that I'm walking backwards to the bed. I feel it against my legs, and he pushes a little harder, knocking me off my feet, onto the bed.

He pulls down my red thong and throws it to the floor. Placing two fingers on my clit, he begins to stroke me.

I moan at how good it feels. It's not just his touch that has me soaring, although it certainly helps. It's the fact that all the worries and the doubts have evaporated into nothing. There is nothing standing between us anymore, and it feels amazing.

He stops, and I open my eyes. He trails his finger down my clit until he finds my aching slit. "Damn," he says, his voice low and deep. "You are so fucking wet."

Then he plunges his finger inside of me. I gasp at the pleasure it sends rippling through my body. He pulls back out and pushes it back in. The steady rhythm is driving me crazy, and my body won't sit still.

I grind my hips against his hand, desperate to feel more. I want to feel all the pleasure he can give me, hard and fast. And I want to come more than anything right now.

I close my eyes again and feel him slide another finger into me. My hands reach for my breasts with a mind of their own, squeezing them and pinching my nipples. My hips writhe on the bed as he strokes me with his fingers, in and out.

He picks up the pace, and I moan louder. He grabs my nipple and pulls.

Sensation grips my entire body, making me dizzy with lust. I breathe in ragged pants with every skilled stroke of his fingers.

He rocks it against me, hard and fast.

It feels so good, and it pushes me closer and closer to the edge. I want to come. I *need* to come.

Then he stops.

My eyes fly open, and I stare at him desperately.

"Sorry, were you close?" he asks with a sly grin.

I know he isn't actually sorry. Otherwise, he would have let me come.

He stands and takes his jacket off, then undoes his tie. Taking his own sweet time while I lie here frustrated. He tosses his tie to the floor and then starts to unbutton his shirt. Desire rages inside me, and the sight of him undressing for me makes it surge more intensely. I want him so badly that I can't just hold back and watch.

I sit up on the edge of the bed and unbuckle his belt for him. I make eye contact with him, and I lick my lips suggestively, making it clear what I'm about to do. I want him to feel the anticipation the way I'm feeling it.

The dark look in his eyes tells me that he's eager.

I unzip his pants and pull them down, followed by his boxer briefs. His cock springs to life in front of me, hard and thick, and I grab it in both hands. I move them up and down, and he grunts at my touch. The sound of it spurs me on, and I stroke harder and faster.

Then I look up at him, open my mouth, and slide my lips over the tip of his cock.

"Fuck, Jade," he groans and places his hand on my head.

I take him deeper into my mouth and then pull back. I do it again, going just a little farther down than before. Then I pull back. I lightly graze his cock with my teeth, a trick I read in a magazine, and I hear him suck in air.

"Goddamn baby," he grunts out.

I open my mouth wide and shove him all the way inside.

Grabbing my hair, he pulls my head back so his cock is barely in my mouth. Then he shoves my head back onto it until he hits the back of my throat. He holds my head in place and starts to thrust in and out of my mouth.

He's moaning and fucking my mouth. It's so hot I'm dripping with excitement.

He lets go of my hair, and I look up at him.

"Lay down," he commands.

I scoot back so my back is lying flat on the bed, and I spread my legs open, exposing myself to his hungry gaze. He rubs my clit with his fingers, and I tremble.

Luke gets onto the bed and positions his cock up against my throbbing pussy. "Do you want it?" he asks.

I nod.

"Tell me how bad you want it," he growls, staring at me like he's about to consume me.

"I want it so fucking bad, Luke, please," I beg. "Please fuck me."

His hips thrust forward, and he buries his entire cock inside of me.

"Oh, my God!" I gasp. The way he fills me up feels so fucking good.

He pulls out and does it again. He repeats this, over and over, until neither one of us can handle it anymore. Then he leans forward and starts thrusting in and out of me with a faster rhythm.

"You feel so damn good," I pant.

"Oh, yeah?" he asks. "You like it when I fuck you?"

"Yes, yes, yes," I moan, my voice breathless.

He moves faster. It's hard and hot, and it's driving me crazy. I can barely think or breathe. My entire world centers down to the two of us, joined together in ecstasy. I'm loving every second of the way he fucks me.

He stops and clasps my legs together, before throwing them over his shoulders. Gripping my ankles tightly, he pushes into me again. I'm tighter because of the way my legs are positioned, and it's harder for him to get inside of me, but it makes him go deeper, and I can feel my pussy squeezing around his cock, gripping onto it and driving him crazy.

"Oh, fuck," he groans and starts to fuck me harder.

I feel myself getting closer. "Don't stop," I moan. "Just like that."

He pounds into me, never letting up, as I get closer and closer until the pressure is too much and I explode. White stars burst in my vision. All of my muscles clench, my pussy throbs and pulses uncontrollably. Pleasure pulses through my entire body in waves, one after the other.

He's still fucking me, but it's gentler as he lets me ride out my climax. "Ready for me?" he asks, gazing down at me.

I nod my head.

"Good. Now get on your hands and knees. I want to take you from behind." He pulls out of me and releases my legs.

I flip over on the mattress and get on all fours, leaning forward and jutting my ass into the air for him. The head of his cock parts my lips, and my pussy clenches with anticipation. He thrusts hard, and I feel him plunge all the way in.

"Fuck," he groans, squeezing my ass.

I bite my lip. He feels so freaking good.

His fingers dig into my hips. It's rough and hot, and I love it. His hips rock faster behind me, pushing harder and farther with every thrust. He's so deep inside of me that it almost hurts, but feels amazing at the same time.

Pausing, Luke grabs my hand and places it on my clit. "Play with yourself," he orders, and slides back inside of me. Gripping my hips, he fucks me hard.

I rub my clit at the same tempo that he's thrusting into me. The combination sends pleasure rocketing through me, and I feel myself getting closer to another orgasm. "Don't stop," I cry out. "Don't stop!"

"Are you gonna come for me again?" he asks.

"Yes." I whimper. I'm getting closer. I move my fingers up and down my clit, faster and faster, as his cock pounds into my pussy.

I'm so close. This feels so incredibly good. I'm about to come again. My body responds to his every movement, and then the intensity of my pleasure consumes me. I fly over the edge, into sweet oblivion. I'm falling and floating at the same time. Sensations surge through me, and I'm bucking and quivering against Luke's body.

I feel him thrust again and again, and suddenly, he stops. He's holding onto me, and I can feel his cock throbbing deliciously inside of me, filling me with wet warmth. We're coming together. The thought makes my orgasm so much better.

He releases my hips just as I'm coming back down, still feeling the aftershocks of pleasure rumble through me. He pulls out and lays down on the bed. I lay beside him, and he pulls me into his arms.

"I want you to know that I'm ready for this," he says. "I love you, and I can't imagine not having you with me."

I smile, more to myself than him since he can't actually see my face. "I love you, too." Contented and happy, I wrap my arm around him and nuzzle my face into his chest. When I woke up this morning, my eyes red from crying, I did not expect my day to turn out this way.

"I won't ever hurt you again," he promises as he leans forward a little and kisses the top of my head.

"I won't ever hurt you, either," I say.

We spend the rest of the day wrapped up in each other, and I can't imagine a better way to spend our final hours in Bangkok.

EPILOGUE

Luke

One year on.

I'm at work, counting the hours, the minutes, and the seconds I have left until the end of the day. I'm stuck in this boring ass meeting, and all I can think about is tonight. I'm nervous, much like I felt last year when Jade and I were in Bangkok together.

I can't believe it's already been a year since I told her how I felt. A year since I actually admitted my feelings, not just to her, but to an auditorium full of the very kind of people who could have laughed at me for being soppy. That's how much I didn't give a shit what anybody else thought of what I chose to do with my life. It's been the best year of my life, and I hope Jade feels the same way. If she doesn't, that means tonight won't go the way I hope it does, but I don't even want to think about that.

The meeting drags on.

I just want it to be over. I could just get up and walk out, but these are some of our best clients, and I know that would look awful. I've just gotta make it another hour and twenty minutes. Or eighty minutes. I like the sound of that better. It sounds shorter that way.

I gave Jade the day off, so I haven't seen her beautiful face since this morning when we woke up. I love living with her. Jade moved in with me six months ago, and we never looked back.

God, I can't believe it's been that long. Time seems to fly by now since we are together. Unlike this fucking meeting. I'm so excited and filled with anticipation about tonight I barely listen.

I remember when we got back to the states. News of Jade and I getting together had reached the company before we did. But except for a few jealous idiots, everybody else was happy for us. They said they knew something was up because I was far too happy since I hired her. I'm amazed that so many other people could see what was building before I did.

Finally, the meeting wraps up, and I practically run out the door. I get strange looks, but I after you've made a fool of yourself in front of hundreds of people these little things don't matter one bit. I grab a taxi and give the driver the address to my penthouse. I slide my hand into my pocket and feel the small velvet box. My heart thumps faster against my ribs. I'm way too nervous. I've got to calm myself down before I give myself away.

Act cool.

Take a deep breath.

Smile.

I repeat the words until we pull up outside of my building. I toss the cabbie a fifty and hear him yell, "Wow! Thanks!"

I rush to the bank of elevators and push the 'up' button. At least five times. I know it won't make it come any faster. I'm just really anxious. I get into the elevator. I never noticed before how long the ride takes to get to the penthouse.

After an age, it dings on our floor, and the doors open. I step out into the penthouse.

Jade comes around the corner. "I thought you said you wanted me ready by five sharp?" she says. "You're fifteen minutes late. I was about to change back into my pajamas."

She's wearing a little blue halter dress I've never seen before. It must be new. I love her in blue. Hell, I love her in every color. Sometimes, I feel like I am in a dream. Then I have to stop and remind myself how lucky I am to have her at all. I almost fucked everything up with her. I can't even imagine how dark and lonely my life would be without her.

She wraps her arms around my neck, and I slide my hands around her hips.

"Sorry, the meeting ran late," I say.

"You probably don't remember anything since your amazing assistant wasn't there."

I kiss her soft lips. "Damn right. I'm completely lost without her."

She grins at me.

"Are you ready?"

She makes a funny face and looks down at her outfit "Are you saying you don't like how I look?"

"You know you blow my mind. I was asking if you are ready to go," I explain.

She smiles. "Yeah, I know. Just the same way you blow mine every single time I see you."

I take her by the hand. Tonight could go one of two ways, but I'm feeling more and more confident that it'll go the way I want it to.

At the restaurant, the hostess leads us to our table in the back. The waitress is right behind her. She takes our drink orders and disappears.

"Can you believe that this time last year, we were in Bangkok?" she asks, her eyes unfocused as she looks into the past.

I smile at her. She thinks we are out celebrating our anniversary. One year of us being together, but it's more than just that. "No. This year has flown by in a flash."

"I can't believe I've put up with your ass for this long," she teases and then winks. Her foot brushes along my leg under the table.

"Are you playing footsy with me, Miss Emerson?"

"I might be playing a few other games a bit later," she promises.

The waitress takes our orders. Jade orders a steak, and I've always loved that she's never been one to order just a salad and sit picking at it. No, she has a healthy appetite which I truly appreciate.

"I love meat," she says and licks her lips, when the waitress leaves. "I can't wait to get all that delicious meat inside of me."

Double entendre. I love that she does that. God, I'm just so in love with her.

Dinner is delicious. The waitress comes around to collect our plates and asks if we want dessert. We politely decline, and I pay the bill.

We stand to leave. I stop and bend over, pretending to tie my shoe.

She's looking around at the people and decorations. I pull the box out of my pocket, flip open the lid, and stare up at her. I'm waiting for her to look back at me. The lady next to us gasps, and that's when Jade looks at me.

"Oh, my God," she says, her hand flying to her mouth.

"Jade, you are the one person that was able to steal my heart. You were that one girl who got me to change my wicked ways. I can't picture my life without you. I wouldn't have a life without you in it."

There are tears in her eyes.

"I love everything about you. From your witty banter to your intelligence. You balance me out and make me whole. I don't ever want to go another day without knowing that you want to spend the rest of your life with me. So...Jade Emerson, will you marry me?"

"Yes!" she yells before she starts to cry.

Someone starts a slow clap, and it turns into a standing ovation from everyone in the dining room.

I slide the ring onto her delicate finger, stand up, and pick her up. Our lips lock. Our tongues are tied. I put her back down, and we pull apart just as the applause ends. I grab her hand, and waving at everyone, we head out of the restaurant.

We grab the first cab we can, and in the back, she's practically sitting on my lap. We can't keep our hands off each other. Desire is thick in the air. I want her so fucking bad, and I can tell she wants me. I put a hand on her leg and slide up until I feel her panties. I move them to the side and slide a finger inside of her. She stays quiet while I start to caress her. I pull my finger out and put it in my mouth. "Mmm, dessert."

Her eyes shine. She smiles.

The cab driver pulls up outside of our building, and once again, I'm in a rush to get out of the cab. I toss him a fifty, and we climb out. We run to the elevators, and are relieved when we are alone in it.

She starts kissing me, as I pick her up and push her against the wall of the elevator. Her legs are wrapped around me. Her arms are wrapped around my neck. Her mouth tastes so good. Soft moans fill my ears.

My dick is hard and pressed against her. I reach up and start to pull her panties off.

"Hey, now," she says. "We're still in the elevator."

"So what?" I kiss her again to drive my point home.

She shrugs, and I pull her panties down. I have to set her down to get them fully off of her, but as soon as they are off and on the floor, I pick her back up. She's grinding against my hard length, and it feels so damn good.

I want this elevator to hurry up so that I can fuck my fiancé.

Finally, I hear the ding. The doors open up, and I carry her to our bedroom. I lay her down on the bed and position her so I can access her pussy.

She spreads her legs. It's hot the way she's lying there. I flick my tongue across the tip of her clit. I've learned where all of her most sensitive areas are, and I'm not afraid to use them to my advantage, I flick my tongue back and forth.

Jade wiggles her hips as she moans and puts her hands in my hair.

I press my tongue harder onto her clit and lick it up and down. She tastes so sweet, so good. I love, love, love eating her.

I take my middle finger and slide it into her hot pussy. I knew she was going to be wet, but I didn't think she was going to be this wet. Her pussy walls are squeezing around my finger. The warmth and wetness from her are driving me crazy. I pull my finger out.

"Take the dress off," I demand.

Standing, she slowly, seductively removes her dress, letting it slide to the floor.

I can't get my clothes off fast enough. I toss my shirt off to the side and then undo my belt and unzip my pants. I yank them down with my boxers. I'm ready to get inside of her and feel her pussy on my cock.

Jade lays back down on the bed and starts to rub her clit.

"Oh, fuck," I groan. "That's so hot."

She bites her plump bottom lip and moans. She knows how crazy it makes me.

It's more than I can handle. I get onto the bed and push her legs apart. I hold my cock in my right hand and press it up against her pussy. I rub it along her clit, and she moans. I move it down to her tight hole, and then I thrust hard so that I slide all the way inside of her.

"Oh, holy hell," she groans.

I start to thrust faster.

"Yes," she encourages.

It's so hot the way she's lying here under me while grabbing onto her tits and squeezing them. And she's so fucking hot. I can't get enough of it. I start fucking her harder and faster. Her breathing is shallow and ragged.

"Are you gonna come for me?" I ask her.

She nods her head, and her moans grow louder.

I stop thrusting and lift her legs up. I place one on each shoulder and shove myself inside of her, hard.

"Oh, fuck!" she cries out.

I thrust hard, and I'm deep inside of her. I can see in her eyes that she's going crazy. She's getting close to an orgasm, and I want to watch her come. I love the look she gets in her eyes when she climaxes. I love it so much I would stay home all day and make her come over and over again just to see it. "Come for me," I urge.

"I'm so close," she moans. "Don't stop."

I move faster and I place my hand on her pussy. I start to rub her clit as I fuck her, and she's grinding her body against my hand. And then I watch as her eyes brighten, and I feel her body tense. She's screaming my name, and it's the sexiest sound I've ever heard.

"That's right, come for me," I say to her.

When she comes down from her orgasm, I tell her to get on top of me.

I pull out and lay on my back. I hold my dick up while she straddles me and lowers herself on. I aim perfectly and slide right inside of her. "Oh fuck," I grunt.

I put my hands on her hips, and she rocks them back and forth. I'm deep inside of her, and her tight pussy is wrapped around my cock. I love when she's on top. She starts to bounce her body up and down, and I can feel myself sliding in and out of her.

"Damn," I moan again. I can't help it because it feels so fucking good.

She pauses what she's doing, leans forward, and grabs onto my biceps. She repositions herself and starts grinding her hips back and forth in a fast motion. "I think I'm gonna come," she says. Just as the sentence ends, I see her eyes light up again, and she starts moaning. Her movements become more intense. She's coming again.

I wrap my arms around the small of her back and pull her down so our chests are touching. I start to thrust myself in and out of her. It feels amazing, and I'm so fucking close.

I want to blow my load inside of her so bad. She's moaning, as I'm fucking her harder and harder, then all of a sudden, all my muscles tense. "Oh, *fuck*," I roar and hold onto her as my climax overpowers my will to do anything else. It's amazing and mind blowing. Everything I've ever wanted it to be.

When I come down, she climbs off of me and rolls next to me. She wraps her leg around mine and throws her arm over my chest. "That was fucking amazing."

"Yeah it was," I reply breathlessly. "Thank you."

She laughs. "What for?"

"For saying yes."

She gazes at her left hand and then props herself up and looks at me. She kisses me and then says, "Thank you for asking me. I mean it only took a year for you to realize you wanted to marry me."

I laugh. "No, that only took an hour."

"Whatever," she scoffs.

"I'm serious. That first night when we had sex, I knew something was different about you. Something that drew me in and made me want to find out more. It's kind of why I freaked out."

"I'm glad you got over yourself," she retorts, smiling.

"Me too," I say and kiss the top of her head.

I know that our life together is going to have its ups and down, but I also know that she's the one for me. And if it wasn't for Bangkok, I never would have realized that the woman who was perfect had been next to me all along.

All I had to do was open my eyes and see her.

Jade
Five years on.

How long has it been since we were last like this? It's hard to remember specifically, especially as Luke grabs my hips and positions me so I'm bent over his conference-room desk.

"You're the best secretary I've ever had, you know that?" He leans down and growls in my ear, running his hand down my naked back. He's still mostly dressed, something I find insanely hot, especially once he's stripped me down to nothing but my heels.

He thrusts into me.

I gasp with pleasure. "I deserve a raise for this," I reply breathily, clenching the table's edge as I shudder with pleasure. Amazing, how he still feels good after all this time.

"Maybe I could tempt you into some supplemental activities," he says, tracing his hand across my ass and landing two sharp slaps across my butt-cheeks. I squeal with pain and pleasure as I grind my ass back against him, driving him deeper inside me.

"Like?"

"I've got a conference to attend in Asia and I could do with a companion," he grunts as he thrusts deep and hard into me." He holds himself there for a second before he finishes the thought. "Someone to keep me satisfied. To give me blowjobs. Someone I could fuck all night long."

"I'm not sure that's possible for just one woman," I shoot back.

He laughs cruelly, wraps my ponytail around his hand, and tugs my head back.

I wince, but I like it when he is dominating. He knows exactly what buttons to push, exactly how hard to go to make it feel incredible. Well, he's spent long enough getting to know this body. I'd hope he knows exactly what turns me on by now.

"You make a fair point," he agrees, as he suddenly withdraws.

Flipping me around and laying me flat on my back, he grabs my leg and drapes it over his shoulder. I watch him kiss the inside of my knee. Mmm…sexy. Then he plunges back into me in one swift motion. My eyes roll back and for some weird reason, I suddenly have a flash of our honeymoon. We'd gone to visit Hawaii. After a few glasses of wine, we snuck into the offices of the Hawaiian branch of Omega and screwed our brains out on pretty much every bit of office furniture we could find. God, it feels like so long ago.

My train of thought-drift returns pretty swiftly when buried deep inside me, he leans down and kisses me. My mouth opens for him and he pushes his tongue in. I grip his hair and pull him even closer. I suck his tongue mindlessly. I'm addicted to the taste of my husband. Have been from the first taste.

"Play with yourself," he murmurs in my ear, flicking his tongue out against my neck as he pushes himself back up on top of me.

I'm a good girl and I do as I'm told, trailing my hand tantalizingly down my stomach as he watches me hungrily. I reach my clit, and begin to masturbate, closing my eyes and lifting my back off the table as I reach whole new levels of ecstasy.

Just as I'm about to crest, I feel his hand cover mine. I open my eyes.

He smiles slowly.

I bite my lip.

He starts thrusting again.

We've been at this for what felt like hours- and I haven't come yet. He hasn't let me.

Not that I mind terribly. I love the build, the slow tease, the passion as he drives me to the edge, and then pulls back again, pushing me as far as I can go before I can take no more.

I know that this time, this is it, there'll be no holding back. I've reached the point of no return and so has he. I see it in his eyes. I recognize that look, as he forces himself to meet my gaze. His teeth are gritted, his hips pounding in time with mine, his hands gripping me tight.

All of a sudden, my orgasm tears through me.

I let out a loud cry, refusing to hold back, my body shuddering from head to toe. A few seconds later, I feel his cock swell inside me as he reaches his own climax. He lets out a loud roar and pushes himself as deep as he can go. My pussy clenches tight around his cock as though I never want him to pull out. Slowly, our breathing returns to normal, and he withdraws out of me.

"Can you pass me my panties?" I ask with a giggle, crossing my arms over my chest in a chaste gesture.

Luke reaches over and pulls my arms apart, planting a kiss on one of my still-hard nipples. "Sure you don't want round two?" he asks.

I have to admit it's tempting, but we have other commitments. "I left Mason with the nanny," I pull a face. "And we really should get back there before her shift finishes."

"Fair point." He shrugs and starts buttoning up his pants. He starts going around and picking up my clothes scattered about the room. He grins as he hands them to me.

I cock my head. "What?"

"This just reminds me of the old days," he notes with a lopsided grin. "When I was your boss."

"Well, that was the point, wasn't it?" I remind him.

He wraps his arms around my waist. "I suppose it is," he agrees. "Which reminds me, when can we pencil this in again?"

"You'll have to check with your secretary," I tease.

"Right," he murmurs and covers my mouth with his.

And I'm once again lost to his embrace.

The End

Made in the USA
Lexington, KY
12 November 2017